The *Heiress Brides*

~TWO NOVELLAS~

PAMELA SHERWOOD

BCP
BLUE CASTLE
PUBLISHING

THE HEIRESS BRIDES contains two previously published novellas, *A Scandal in Newport* and *A Wedding in Cornwall*

Excerpts from *Waltz with a Stranger* and *A Song at Twilight*

Copyright © 2016 Pamela Sherwood
Published by Blue Castle Publishing
Cover by AMDesignStudios.net

ISBN-13; 978-0-9908612-2-5

For my readers, especially the print lovers who inspired this collection

CONTENTS

A Scandal in Newport   1

A Wedding in Cornwall   103

Thank You   167
Waltz with a Stranger: Excerpt   169
A Song at Twilight: Excerpt   179
Acknowledgments   183
Also by Pamela Sherwood   185
About the Author   187

A SCANDAL IN NEWPORT

PROLOGUE

Stone walls do not a prison make,
Nor iron bars a cage...
—RICHARD LOVELACE, "To Althea: From Prison"

NEWPORT, *September 1891*

HE'D TAKEN HER RING, the swine.

Shifting uncomfortably on the hard mattress beneath her, Amy glared down at the circle of bare skin on the third finger of her left hand. Easy enough to understand why it had been taken, but it still made her want to scream with rage.

Not that she *could* right now, thanks to the gag. And she suspected that, even without the gag, no one would be able to hear her if she screamed. What had Geneva told her? A room with all the windows boarded up—in an abandoned building, most likely.

Amy shifted position again, as best she could. The ropes were tight about her wrists, even tighter about her ankles. Trussed up like a Thanksgiving turkey... perhaps if she wriggled about enough, she could manage to loosen her bonds—or at least lessen the horrid "pins and needles" sensation growing in her feet.

In that latter aim, she managed to succeed, and lay quietly until her feet stopped tingling. Her mind, however, was far from quiet, furiously turning over the events of the previous night.

Had Sally gotten away? She prayed the younger girl had had the sense to run back into the ballroom, in the direction of light and noise and *people*. Her heart gave a sudden lurch at the thought of *her* people. Mama. Papa. Andrew. Even Relia, far off in Cornwall. And Thomas.

Oh, dear God, *Thomas*. He must know by now—and he'd be *frantic*. Just as her family would be. She could see his face in her mind's eye, strained and taut, his beautiful eyes gone that muddy green they always became in times of intense disquiet.

So outwardly self-contained, the man she loved. And so passionate, so unexpectedly vulnerable, beneath his polished surface...

A wave of longing washed over her, and she shut her eyes against the unwelcome sting of tears. No, she wasn't going to cry. She was far too angry to cry, then or now.

Best to keep a cool head. To remember what she'd already discovered about these kidnappings. Had the ransom demand come yet? And how long would it take for Papa to get such a sum together?

No fear that he would, of course. That was why her captors had started this filthy business in the first place. Rich men's daughters, sheltered, trusting, and naïve. No more able to fend for themselves than babes in the wood. As Alice, Geneva, and poor Maisie had been.

Her lips formed a grim smile about the gag. They'd gotten more than they bargained for when they snatched *her*. She only hoped that some of her scratches had drawn blood, and that at least one of the swine had black and blue shins from all the kicks she'd dealt him as they hustled her off. They'd probably be all too glad to get her off their hands.

She had only to wait, after all. Two days, three at the most—if she couldn't find a way out of this predicament by herself, before then. *Keep a cool head*, Amy told herself. A cool head and all her wits about her, and she'd come out of this all right.

But in spite of her resolve, she found her gaze still straying to her now-bare finger, and her thoughts drifting as well. Back to the night Thomas had put that ring on her finger.

The happiest night of her life...

CHAPTER ONE

Look how my ring encompasseth thy finger,
Even so thy breast encloseth my poor heart;
Wear both of them, for both of them are thine.
—WILLIAM SHAKESPEARE, *King Richard III*

RICHMOND, *July 1891*

AS THE STRAINS of "The Blue Danube" waltz filled the ballroom, Amy's spirits soared to the height of the high, arched ceiling, its azure expanse scattered with tiny, glittering silver stars. Indeed, if such a thing were possible, she thought she could rise and float up there with them.

Except that she had no wish to be any place other than where she was just now. Dancing in Thomas Sheridan's arms, at Havenhurst—his mother's Richmond estate, on the night of their betrothal ball.

She glanced up at him through her lashes, saw him smile in response, that rare, unguarded smile he allowed so few people to see. And warmth eddied around her heart at the knowledge that she was among that privileged few.

Well-defended, her Thomas—as she herself was. Or had been until they met. But together... they were free to be something more.

Our true selves, perhaps. There was only one other person in Amy's life with whom she'd ever felt she could be so unguarded —her twin sister, Aurelia.

And Relia was here tonight, dancing with *her* fiancé James, Earl of Trevenan, their wedding just a fortnight away. That he'd recently been engaged to Amy, before discovering his greater affection for her twin, could have been a cause for gossip— were it not for the perfect amity between the three of them. Besides, everyone was *much* better suited as they were, Amy reflected with what she hoped was a forgivable degree of complacency.

"Is it possible to be drunk on happiness?" she asked dreamily, as Thomas led her into a graceful turn that set her jonquil-yellow skirts swirling about them both.

His mouth quirked up. "Perhaps—metaphorically, if not literally. Do you believe yourself to be in that extraordinary condition?"

Amy laughed. "Believe? I *know*, Mr. Sheridan! And what's more," she lowered her voice so he had to stoop to hear her, "I wouldn't trade it for any other feeling in the world."

His eyes warmed to a brilliant green, and he contrived to draw her closer within the circle of his arms. Amy smiled and rested her head against his shoulder, breathing in the scents of citrus, sandalwood, and him. And why not? They were betrothed, after all.

When the waltz ended, Thomas led her from the floor, towards the French windows opening onto the terrace. "I thought we might—take some air," he explained. "Unless you'd prefer to dance again?"

Amy shook her head. "The next is a Lancers, and I left that unclaimed on purpose. Besides," she leaned with a smile into the circle of his arm, "do you really think I'd pass up the opportunity to be alone with you tonight?"

His smile this time held a faint glimmer of mischief that

made her pulse quicken agreeably. "I rather hoped you'd say that," he murmured, and escorted her onto the terrace.

A balmy summer night, scented with roses and jasmine—like the perfume blended just for her, which was lovely but still not quite as exhilarating as the flowers themselves, Amy decided, inhaling deeply. But then, Havenhurst always smelled like a garden in bloom, which was one of its attractions.

Promenading on Thomas's arm, she found herself remembering her previous visit to Havenhurst. Just four short months ago, she'd experienced what she thought of as one of her greatest humiliations here. Now, however, she could look back on that afternoon with amazement and wonder. Who'd ever have thought matters would turn out like this? And that she'd be celebrating her betrothal—to a son of the house, no less—in this very place?

She glanced up at Thomas, to find him looking back at her, his expression tender yet knowing. Following the train of her thought, as he so often did. But then, he would remember that afternoon too—a turning point for him as well as for her.

"Amelia." And how she loved the way he spoke her full name, the undulant caress of his voice against those four syllables! "Has this evening been all that you could wish?"

"All and more. I wasn't sure how your family would receive me—one of those brazen American pirates," she smiled to take the sting out of those words, "but everyone here has been so kind. Especially your mother!"

"I think she's simply relieved at this point to see me marry at all. And to someone she actually considers—suitable."

As opposed to some of the women with whom he'd previously kept company, Amy translated without difficulty. But then, marriage had never been the goal with any of them, she knew. Unlike Elizabeth, Thomas's first betrothed, who'd died of a fatal chill ten years ago. That tragedy had burned into his soul, convincing him that he could neither love nor wish to love with such intensity again.

Amy had once held a similar view herself—that love was worth neither the risk nor the potential heartache. But now here they were, she and Thomas: two guarded hearts, learning to open up to each other. Two wary people unexpectedly caught up into love.

Worth the risk? *Beyond a doubt, yes.*

"Thomas," she began, as they leaned side by side against the marble balustrade. "I was just wondering. Everyone else calls me Amy, but I am always Amelia to you—why is that?"

"Ah." He paused, his expression contemplative. "Well, in your case, Amy is the diminutive form, is it not? Pretty enough as such, but, if you'll pardon my saying so, I find it a bit… slight. And I don't think of *you* as slight."

Amy blinked, feeling as though she'd been complimented in some obscure way. "How do you think of me, then?'

His eyes crinkled at the corners. "As a force of nature!" Above her astonished laughter, he added, "And 'Amelia' means 'industrious,' which I find very fitting. But do you dislike your given name?"

"Not exactly. It's just that—well, it was my grandmother's name first," she explained. "She lived with us for a number of years, so I shortened it to Amy, to avoid confusion." She pulled a face. "It seemed preferable to being called 'Little Amelia' for the rest of my life!"

"Understandable. And if you would prefer me to address you as Amy—"

She shook her head, smiling. "I don't mind being *your* Amelia. In fact, I rather like your having a name for me that no one else uses!"

"Do you indeed? Well, as it happens, I have something else for you as well," he told her. "Something you should have had much sooner from me."

"Oh?" Amy regarded him quizzically. "And what might that be?"

"Close your eyes and hold out your left hand."

Mystified, she obeyed, felt him gently tug off her evening glove, and then slide something cool onto her third finger.

Understanding dawned, bright as a midsummer bonfire. And her eyes flew open at once, lighting upon the ring she now wore.

Like nothing she'd ever seen. Certainly not like the ring she'd been given during her first betrothal. A sparkling yellow stone—a diamond, she was sure of it—rested between the horns of what looked like a crescent moon, and a swirl of tinier diamonds, clear ones this time, encircled the whole.

Marveling, Amy lifted her gaze to her fiancé's face to find him watching her intently.

"I couldn't decide what to give you," he explained. "The family heirlooms seemed too heavy and outmoded. And nothing I saw at the jewelers' looked right. In the end… I decided to design something myself."

"You *designed* this for me? My ring is… one of a kind?"

"As unique as its wearer," he confirmed. "Do you like it?"

"Oh, *yes*," Amy breathed, holding up her hand and turning it to make the diamonds flash. "And even more now." She frowned a little, trying to recall what jewel lore she knew. "And it… means something, doesn't it, your design?"

He relaxed, the smile she loved dawning first in his eyes. "Very perceptive of you, sweetheart."

"It's not a question of perception, so much as it is of knowing *you*," Amy countered, smiling back. "You're a conundrum, Thomas Sheridan! Almost nothing about you is simple or straightforward!" And thank goodness for that, she thought, as it promised a lifetime of exciting discoveries for them both. "So tell me, what *is* the riddle of my ring?"

"Oh, it's not so difficult to decipher," he began, then relented as she shook her fist at him. "Well, as you know, I am unlikely ever to have a title—"

"I don't care about that—"

"Or a grand estate—"

"I don't care about that, either—"

"But, in my own fashion," Thomas continued, taking Amy's left hand and touching each stone on her ring in turn, "I wished to give you… the sun, the moon, and the stars."

"*Ohhh…*" The breath went out of her in a long, shaky sigh, and the ring on her finger became a watery blur.

Thomas's gaze sharpened. "Amelia, sweetheart, are you—"

The breath went out of him in a huff as she threw her arms about his neck and kissed him fiercely. Almost at once, his own arms came up to enfold her, close and warm, as he returned her kiss with an ardor quite at odds with the cool demeanor he habitually showed to Society.

"You Americans," he murmured against her hair. "So demonstrative."

"You English," she retorted, not a whit deceived. "So eternally po-faced!" Framing his face with her hands, she gazed up into his beautiful green eyes. "Thomas Sheridan, you are the most amazing, chivalrous, romantic man I have ever known!"

His brows rose. "Am I indeed? Well, don't tell anyone, or my reputation will be sunk beyond recovery."

"Your secret is safe with me," she promised, and leaned in for another kiss that would seal their pact.

There was a light feminine cough behind them, and they instinctively pulled apart, their heads turning in the direction of the sound.

"Pardon me for interrupting, Miss Newbold, Thomas." Lady Warrender, one of Society's most fashionable young matrons, stood a few feet away, smiling at them tentatively but with genuine warmth. "I haven't had the chance to speak to you before, but... I wanted to wish you both happy."

Amy relaxed, smiling back. "Thank you, Lady Warrender." Thomas's late betrothed had been Lady Warrender's older sister, and she and Thomas remained good friends. It was a very good sign indeed that she appeared to support his engagement.

"Oh, call me Eleanor, please," the baroness insisted. "And I do hope you'll consider me your friend as well as Thomas's!"

"I should like that very much," Amy told her, further touched by this sign of acceptance. She and Lady Warrender had always been cordial, but this was sweeter still. "And I am Amy."

"Well, then... Amy, may I presume upon an old friendship and borrow Thomas from you, just for a few minutes?"

Her tone was casual but Amy caught the faint note of urgency in her voice. "Certainly, Eleanor." She touched

11

Thomas's hand in a fleeting caress. "I'll be inside, showing my ring to Relia," she told him.

"I'll join you presently," he promised, smiling in the way she loved.

Reassured, Amy headed back to the ballroom, leaving the childhood friends to their private exchange.

~

ALONE IN THE MOONLIGHT, Thomas studied his almost-sister-in-law. "I am glad you came tonight, Eleanor."

She smiled, looking so like Elizabeth for a moment that his heart gave a painful little start. "I wouldn't have missed it. You know that, dear."

He smiled wryly. "I imagine you think it's high time I settled down?"

"Oh, past time." She touched his hand to take any sting out of her words. "I've been worried about you, these past ten years. All those—intrigues, and I know you didn't care a straw for any of those women," she added with the frankness of which only a childhood friend is capable. "I don't know that *I* would have chosen Miss Newbold for you myself, not without a deeper acquaintance than we've enjoyed so far. But sometimes the heart knows best, doesn't it?"

"In this case, the heart… turned out to be considerably wiser than the head," he admitted. There'd been a time not so long ago when he'd firmly believed Amelia to be out of his reach, a woman whose beauty, spirit, and charm he could only admire in the abstract—as an artist would, a woman who could never be his. Fortunately, *she* had had other ideas, which he'd found himself unwilling and unable to resist.

"And you are happy, Thomas?" Eleanor asked, her eyes searching his eyes.

"Yes," he said with conviction. "Remarkably so."

"Good. That's all I wanted for you. What *she* would want for you."

Elizabeth. For a moment their thoughts sped backwards, to

their shared tragedy. To a nightmarish train journey from Oxford to Devonshire... and a greater nightmare awaiting him at the end. It would have been just as difficult for Eleanor, though, watching helplessly with the rest of her family as her beloved sister slipped away. Except that she'd had the chance to say goodbye...

He said with difficulty, forcing words past a sudden tightness in his throat. "It's always— haunted me, that I didn't reach her in time. That she was gone before I arrived."

She caught his hands in hers, squeezing them gently. "Hush— you came as quickly as you could. And there was nothing you could have done! Pneumonia is like that, the doctors say. Horribly swift—but at least she did not suffer in the end."

So they'd told him at the time—and he'd always wondered if that had been a kind lie, meant to console the otherwise inconsolable. But he wished it had been true for Elizabeth's sake. that at the last, she'd simply fallen asleep in one world, to wake again in the next. "I loved her."

The declaration came out husky and not entirely steady.

"I know." Eleanor lowered her head to brush a kiss across his knuckles.

He took a breath. "And—I love Amelia too. Being with her is like... seeing the sun again, after a week of rain."

She nodded, her eyes brimming but a faint smile curving her lips. "Then, I'm happy—truly happy—for you." She cleared her throat and said more briskly, "So, have you set a wedding date? Your family's been remarkably close-mouthed about the details so far."

"Amelia's doing—she's determined not to steal her sister's thunder. But we're planning on an autumn wedding—late October or early November—in New York." He smiled. "She would very much like a grand affair, and I'm of a mind to indulge her."

"Very uxorious of you!" she teased. "So, you'll be going over soon, I imagine?"

"Right after James and Aurelia's wedding. Amelia is convinced I'll find New York artistically stimulating—and she could be right. But most of society will be in Newport for the summer, so we'll be spending some weeks there as well."

"I've heard Newport can be lovely at this time of year, though I've never been there. You must write and let me know how you find it."

"Very well. And I'm sure Amelia would also be glad to write you."

"Talking of whom, I've kept you from her quite long enough," Eleanor said. "And Warrender probably wonders where I've disappeared to, as well. Let's go back inside."

"With pleasure." He offered his arm and they left the terrace together.

Within moments of their reentering the ballroom, Lord Warrender materialized to reclaim his wife and whisk her off for the set starting to form on the dance floor. Looking around for his fiancée, Thomas spied her in a quiet corner with her twin, both of them admiring Amelia's ring. James stood behind Aurelia's chair, watching the sisters with undisguised affection.

Amelia's face brightened when she saw him approach, and she rose with alacrity to meet him. No Englishwoman would have shown her eagerness to be with him so openly, he mused, and while some might find such behavior forward, *he* found it deeply flattering—even satisfying, in a curiously primal way. There was indeed something to be said for American directness.

"Well, sweetheart, did your sister approve?" he asked, offering his arm.

"Completely." Again she held out her hand to admire the play of light on the stones in her ring. "She was especially impressed to learn you'd designed it yourself. *And* she thinks we'll be very happy together."

"I think I've managed to convince Eleanor of the same thing," he told her.

"Have you? Oh, I'm so glad! I know she very much *wants* you to be happy. Would the Warrenders come to our wedding, do you think?"

He considered the matter, then nodded. "Yes, I believe they'd be willing to make the crossing for it. By the way, Eleanor would also like it if we both wrote to her about Newport, as she's never been there."

"No? Well, then, I'll be sure to do so. Not that there will be much to report, besides some Society gossip," she added, shrugging. "Nothing *really* dramatic ever happens in Newport. Shall we go and join the dancers? I think they're setting up for a polka now."

"It would be my pleasure," Thomas replied, leading her onto the dance floor.

~

New York, 12 August 1891

Dearest Relia,

I write this in the complete expectation that you're unlikely to read this until you return from your honeymoon, which I hope you are enjoying to the fullest. And I have no doubt that James is doing his utmost to ensure that very result!

Our crossing was uneventful, the weather fine, and the sea as smooth as glass for most of the voyage. I did have to retire to my stateroom for the first few days. Not from mal de mer—just the usual monthly inconvenience. Fortunately, I made a quick recovery, quicker than the last time. Thomas says it must have been the sea air, but I prefer to think it was Thomas himself and simply not wanting to waste any time we might have to spend together.

I can see you smiling, Relia, and I can't blame you one bit! I held out such a long time against love, and now here I am: head over heels. And I think—I hope—it's the same for Thomas, even though he hides his deeper feelings so well. In any case, we had a lovely time, strolling together on the promenade deck and watching dolphins frolic from the rail. Thomas wanted to sketch them, and managed to capture some of their leaping motion, though he considers the finished sketches too rough to be shown to anyone at present. (He sketched me as well, and declared the result far more satisfactory.) My one regret is that I could not, alas, tempt him into any display of affections more intimate than a kiss, but that was probably due to Mama's frequent presence. I have every hope of changing that, now that we're no longer at sea!

Anyway, we arrived in New York three days ago, and tomorrow we leave for Newport. I know that you have completely switched your allegiance to Cornwall, but you must admit that Newport is beautiful in the summer, and I'm looking forward to seeing dear Shore House again. And even our friends—and we did have some true ones, like the Livingstons and the Russells, as opposed to those dratted Vandermeres. And there's Bailey's Beach, the Cliff Walk, and the Casino—all of which I can now share with Thomas. I can hardly wait to see what he makes of the place, as he's never had the opportunity to visit it before. (He likes New York, by the way—the energy appeals to him—and he went off yesterday and the day before to sketch in some places you and I were never allowed to venture.)

But I'd bet you my newest parasol that those Fifth Avenue harridans who used to snub Mama will be fawning all over her now, wanting to know every detail of your wedding to James and what it's like to have an earl for a son-in-law! And I daresay there will be a lot of interest in Thomas as well—and not just from Newport's pushy mamas!

He assures me, however, that he is mine alone—not that I require such assurances, but it's beyond sweet to hear. As I am sure you already know, dearest.

I'll write again, from Newport.

All my love to you and James,
Amy

CHAPTER TWO

Retired to their tea and scandal, according to their ancient custom.
—WILLIAM CONGREVE, *The Double Dealer*

NEWPORT, *August 1891*

"THIS IS WHAT YOU CALL A *COTTAGE*?"

Amy suppressed a smile at the incredulity in Thomas's voice. It wasn't often she saw him nonplussed. "Perhaps 'cottage' might be understating it, a bit?"

"More than a bit." His bemused gaze traveled over the palatial sitting room of the Newbolds' summer home, taking in the pretty marquetry tables and the Louis Quatorze chairs. "I was expecting something considerably smaller, possibly with a thatched roof. Not something that could hold its own with one of England's great houses."

"Oh, Shore House isn't anywhere near as grand as Blenheim or Castle Howard!" Amy protested, though she had always loved her family's pretty Georgian-style manor house and felt secretly pleased by the compliment. "It's actually quite modest, compared to some of the places here. Wait until you see the Ogdens' new house, The Cliffs. We're dining there tonight."

He raised a quizzical brow, stretching out his long legs as they sat down upon the sofa together. "Now, are the Ogdens good friends or mere acquaintances?"

"Somewhere in between. Which describes many of our Newport neighbors, I suppose," Amy confessed with a wry smile.

Sympathy kindled in his eyes. "You've mentioned before that life here—wasn't always easy for your family. I gather Newport society tends to be more exclusive than most?"

"Highly exclusive," she confirmed. "And we were—well, not shunned exactly. Papa's family name was old enough, if Mama's money was comparatively new. And some of our neighbors even became good friends to us. But I did… sometimes feel—among the highest sticklers—that we were included at parties and dinners only on sufferance."

He took her hand, a rare demonstrative gesture for an Englishman. "A wretched way to feel. I've seen some society dragons in London spread just that sort of misery among young ladies desperately trying to fit in. I hope you did not take it too much to heart."

Amy squeezed his hand in reassurance. "I tried not to. I mostly minded for Mama's sake." Laura Newbold was as much of a lady as any born within the Four Hundred, and Amy's blood had always boiled at the grudging acceptance and occasional snub meted out to her mother by the more snobbish Knicker-bocker matrons. "Although," she added with a mischievous smile, "I'm sure her stock has risen considerably, now that one daughter's married to an earl and the other's engaged to a famous artist *and* a duke's grandson!"

Thomas's brows rose again. "Is this to be a triumphal proces-sion, then? Should I walk behind the carriage tonight in chains, like a spoil of war?"

His tone was light, but Amy glanced at him more closely. She'd learned some time ago that Thomas's levity could mask any number of more complicated emotions. Drat the man—he *knew* she loved him for himself and not his birth... or his talent, prodigious though it was!

Fortunately, his eyes held amusement rather than pique or hurt. Relieved, she drew his hand, still linked with hers, up to her cheek and held it there. "No, I want you *in* the carriage, right beside me. Exactly where you belong."

"An excellent reply," he said gravely, and kissed her.

"So, is The Cliffs a bigger house than The Sands?" Thomas asked, some hours later as the Newbolds' carriage rolled smoothly along Bellevue Avenue. "Because cliffs are bigger, generally speaking. Or is The Sands considered bigger, because there's more sand than cliff?"

Amy stifled a giggle. "Oh, hush! We're almost there, and I'll never keep a straight face if you go on like this!"

His eyes crinkled at her. "I merely wished to know how one keeps from confusing all these houses with remarkably similar names. The Cliffs. The Sands. The Dunes. The Tides."

"Thomas has a point," Amy's father observed mildly. "Especially as Newport residents make a practice of trying to outdo each other on general principle. Not only are most houses here similarly named, several have been designed by the same architect. A fellow by the name of Hunt."

"Richard Morris Hunt," Amy's mother confirmed. "He's just finished The Cliffs after more than three years of work! At least, that's what Lucy Ogden told me. And I hear he's now working on a summer home for the William K. Vanderbilts, which will have *fifty* rooms!"

"Fifty!" Amy echoed, startled. "Good heavens!"

"Nothing like living modestly, is there?" Thomas murmured.

Amy choked back another giggle just as they approached the curving drive to The Cliffs. She had the satisfaction of seeing her fiancé's brows rise and hearing his faint intake of breath as he took in the edifice rising before them. But the Ogdens' new residence had been designed along the lines of a French château,

lofty and majestic, so such a reaction was not unwarranted...
even from an English aristocrat effortlessly at home wherever
he went!

Thomas wasn't the only one impressed by The Cliffs. Amy
saw her mother's hand tighten on her father's arm once they'd
descended from the carriage. And Adam Newbold, not always
the most demonstrative of men, patted his wife's hand reassuringly as they headed towards the steps. Amy could admit to a
certain flutter of apprehension herself, but *only* to herself. It was
just a house, after all, albeit a very grand one, to which they'd
been openly invited. She tilted her chin a little higher, glad that
they all looked their best tonight: Thomas and her father in
impeccably tailored black-and-white, Mama and herself in lilac
and peach silk organza, respectively.

Once they were inside, a footman in dark blue livery
escorted them into a grand salon—all frescoes and Italian
artwork—where Mrs. Ogden, regal in oyster silk and pearls, was
holding court among what looked like some two dozen guests.
Amy felt her smile congeal when she recognized an all too
familiar face in the crowd: Sally Vandermere, flanked by her
parents. The same parents whose graciousness towards the
Newbolds had always been tinged with condescension and who
—Amy had no doubt—had encouraged their son to break with
Relia after the riding accident that had lamed her.

Amy darted a glance about the room. Well, at least Stupid
Charlie didn't appear to be of the party tonight. Relia might
regret having caused her faithless former sweetheart pain by
rejecting his renewed courtship in Cornwall, but Amy had no
such compunctions. Charlie's loss was James's gain. Still, she
conceded grudgingly, there was no real harm in Sally herself.
She'd always been as friendly and guileless as a puppy, sure that
she would be liked everywhere she went. And being reasonably
pretty, wealthy, and impeccably placed in New York society, she
certainly wasn't *disliked*! Amy could only hope that Sally's attention would be diverted elsewhere this evening, so they needn't
interact much. Or better yet, not at all. There were several
attractive young men in attendance, including Mrs. Ogden's son

Tony, who might provide an excellent distraction for a young lady so recently out.

Thomas caught her eye and sent her a faint smile: he knew exactly how she felt about the Vandermeres and why. Returning his smile, Amy felt some of her annoyance subside. No matter how aggravating a situation, everything became more bearable when you had someone who understood, she reflected. And only Relia understood her better than Thomas!

Mrs. Ogden spotted them at that moment and approached with outstretched hands and a benevolent smile. "Ah, Laura," she greeted Amy's mother. "So delighted to see you. Welcome back to Newport, my dear."

Better and better. Amy's lingering irritation drained away at their hostess's welcome and her mother's visible pleasure in it. Perhaps, despite the Vandermeres' presence, this evening would be a success, after all.

$\sim$

DINNER WAS UNQUESTIONABLY A SUCCESS: five sumptuous courses prepared by a French chef and served up in a palatial dining room worthy of Versailles. Better still, Amy found herself seated far away from any of the Vandermeres. Her only disappointment was that Thomas was not seated beside her, but she could at least see him and occasionally catch his eye across the table. And there was a certain pleasure in watching him from afar: the light from the chandelier gilding his leaf-brown hair and illuminating his angular features, that bred-in-the-bone elegance that was so much more distinctive than mere good looks.

Not that he didn't look a perfect treat in evening dress. Every inch the aristocrat, in fact, and more than one young lady present eyed him with appreciation and speculative interest. *Eat your hearts out, my dears—he's mine.*

As if he could sense her thoughts, Thomas looked up from his plate and glanced in her direction. Their eyes met, his brilliantly green in the lamplight, and his sculpted mouth curved in a faint smile that sent a pulse of heat through her. Especially when she thought about that mouth pressed against her own—and other sensitive parts of her anatomy. Thomas might be adamant about waiting until their wedding night, but he'd no object to a certain amount of experimentation before then, and he was nothing if not... inventive.

Given the drift of her imaginings, it was probably just as well that Mrs. Ogden rose from the table a few minutes later. Demurely lowering her eyes, Amy accepted the footman's assistance in extricating herself from her heavy brocaded chair, then followed the rest of the ladies out of the dining room.

Mrs. Ogden's parlor was smaller but nearly as grand, its walls papered in flowered silk and its furniture agleam with polish. Much to Amy's amusement, once all the ladies were comfortably settled, their hostess turned her attention to Amy's mother, pressing her for details of Aurelia's wedding.

"Was it very well-attended?" she asked. "Your new son-in-law's an earl, after all."

Laura Newbold smiled. "Well enough, though Cornwall is quite far removed from London. James and Aurelia both wanted a quiet, simple ceremony—he much prefers the country to the town."

"As Relia herself does," Amy chimed in. "But it was a beautiful wedding all the same, just right for them."

"Do you also mean to marry in England, Amy?" Mrs. Ogden inquired, regarding her with renewed interest. "I understand that your fiancé has aristocratic connections too."

"Actually, *my* wedding will be in New York this autumn. Early November. Thomas's family are making the crossing for it, and James and Relia too." Amy was determined to have her twin as an attendant, though there would be other bridesmaids as well.

"We're holding a ball at Shore House in two weeks' time to celebrate the engagement," Mrs. Newbold added with pardonable pride. "I hope you and your family will be able to attend."

"We should be delighted, dear Laura," Mrs. Ogden replied,

beaming. "Indeed, I suspect all of Newport will be clamoring for an invitation!"

Amy hid a smile when she saw her mother blush, just a little. Sweet satisfaction, after years of semi-grudging acceptance! Never underestimate the power of having two daughters connected to the English aristocracy...

"Talking of the rest of Newport, are the Livingstons here this summer?" Mrs. Newbold inquired with an attempt at nonchalance. "I was looking forward to seeing them. Indeed, I am surprised not to see them here tonight."

Mrs. Ogden's eyes widened. "Oh, my heavens—you won't have heard!"

Amy felt her scalp prickle at the hushed horror in the older woman's voice.

"Heard what?" Mrs. Newbold asked, her expression mirroring Amy's unease.

Mrs. Ogden lowered her voice and leaned forward in her chair. "It happened last autumn in New York, while you were abroad. *Three* young ladies, just in their first season, kidnapped and held for ransom: Alice Carr, Maisie Van Allen, and Geneva Livingston!"

Kidnapped? Amy stifled a gasp as her mother exclaimed, "How dreadful! Were they all taken together?"

"Oh, no—one at a time," Mrs. Ogden clarified. "Apparently, each was waylaid at night, while returning from a social engagement. Ransom notes were delivered within a day—I have no idea how much was demanded, but the families paid, of course."

Of course. Having some acquaintance with all three families, Amy knew there was no question but that the girls' fathers, among the wealthiest in New York, would part with any sum to have their daughters back safe and sound.

"But what about the police?" Mrs. Newbold asked. "Weren't *they* able to help?"

Mrs. Ogden shook her head. "The police weren't contacted until the girls were freed—that was one of the conditions for their safe return. They were brought in, afterwards, but despite their best efforts, they haven't yet discovered the kidnappers.

And the girls had been kept bound and in the dark most of the time so they couldn't provide much information."

"But they *were* released unharmed?"

"Well, none of them appeared to be injured, but such an ordeal leaves its mark." Mrs. Ogden fanned herself vigorously. "Poor Maisie fared the worst. She suffered a terrible asthma attack after being rescued and nearly died of it. Then, after... well, I've heard she's still fragile, and the Van Allens thought it best for her to recover in more—peaceful surroundings."

A sanatorium, Amy translated with a shiver. Poor Maisie, indeed.

"The Carrs have taken Alice abroad this summer," Mrs. Ogden continued in hushed tones. "But the Livingstons have brought Geneva to Newport—they just aren't accepting many invitations at present. All the same, it must be a relief for them to be away from the city!" She glanced towards her own daughter, presently conversing with Sally Vandermere and a few other young ladies. "I'd have been beside myself if something like this had happened to Mabel!"

"Any mother who loves her daughter would be!" Mrs. Newbold agreed with a shudder. "I can't be sorry to have missed that. Have there been other attempts since?"

"No, thank goodness! The kidnappings stopped as suddenly as they started—" Mrs. Ogden broke off at the sound of approaching male voices. "The men are coming to join us. Let us have some more *pleasant* conversation now, shall we?"

~

"I KNEW ALL OF THEM," Amy told Thomas later that evening as they sat together in the private parlor adjoining her room, her parents having retired for the night. "The Livingstons chiefly, but the other two families were just as prominent, and we were always seeing them—at dances and dinner parties, and whatnot. What a terrible thing to happen to those girls, and in their first Season too!"

"Terrible indeed." Setting aside his sketchbook, Thomas put a comforting arm around her. "Especially to poor Miss Van Allen."

Amy suppressed a shiver. "I was least acquainted with Maisie, but I'd heard that she didn't enjoy the most robust of health, and that she suffered dreadfully from asthma."

His mouth flattened into a grim line. "I knew a boy at school who was similarly afflicted. And it always got worse when he was agitated or frightened. Her abductors may not have intended her harm, but beyond a doubt, they should be held accountable for her breakdown."

"Instead, they got away with their crime—repeatedly," Amy observed with disgust. "Given how successful they were at this filthy business, I'm surprised they stopped after only three. Relieved but still surprised."

"Have they, though?" Thomas mused, frowning.

"Mrs. Ogden said there have been no further abductions since Maisie's, in January. The city was on edge all winter, but no one else was taken. She also said the police are still investigating the crime, but they've yet to find a trace of the kidnappers. Which seems to argue that they've run off somewhere to enjoy their ill-gotten gains."

"Or that they're lying low, waiting for another opportunity to strike."

Amy shuddered. "What a horrifying thought!"

"Forgive me for sounding alarmist, sweetheart, but criminals seldom stop once they find a gambit that works for them," he pointed out. "So far, every family whom they've targeted has complied with their demands: no police and the ransoms paid in full. Easy pickings—it's hard to imagine them giving that up. The only positive is that the police might know what to expect by now, if they *do* try again."

Amy leaned into his encircling arm. "Another reason to be glad we're out of New York right now. Newport has its faults, but at least there's nothing to fear here. Except perhaps the usual society dragons and an excess of social climbing."

His mouth quirked. "I imagine some people find those quite terrifying enough."

"I'd like to call on the Livingstons tomorrow," Amy said decisively. "They were always decent to us—much nicer than some of the other families in the Four Hundred."

"Friendlier than the Ogdens?"

"Well, more *genuine* about it," she clarified. "I suppose it helped that Venetia was two years older than Relia and I, and she was safely engaged before we came out. And Geneva's three years younger than us, so we've never been in direct competition with any of the Livingston girls. Anyway, Mrs. Livingston was among those who never looked down on my mother, so for that reason alone, I'd have appreciated her. Mrs. Ogden says the family isn't accepting many invitations right now, but I'd still like to ask them to our engagement ball. And let Geneva know that she'll be safe among friends."

His eyes warmed. "You have a generous nature, Amelia. It's one of your finest qualities."

"Thank you, sir." She smiled as she pressed closer yet to him. "Would you like me to show you just *how* generous I can be?"

He stilled, as she trailed her fingers through his fine leaf-brown hair, traced the whorl of his earlobe, stroked the nape of his neck—and felt his slight shiver of response. One delicious secret she'd discovered: Thomas was ticklish, though he would deny it to his last breath.

A game between them, and one of the most delightful Amy had ever played. Her fiancé was so determined not to consummate their love before the wedding night, at which point he promised her all manner of earthly delights. But it was rather like being told that dinner was three hours off when one was famished!

He turned suddenly with that speed that always surprised her in him, and caught her to him, his mouth claiming hers. Exultant, Amy returned his kiss, relishing the press of his lean, angular frame flush against hers. *So* much better than on board the ship, and without Mama or Papa there to interrupt!

She linked her arms about Thomas's neck and had to suppress a triumphant exclamation when he swept her up in his arms, as though she weighed no more than a child, then rose from the sofa and crossed the room in a few swift strides.

Nudging open the door to her chamber (and thank goodness she'd had the foresight to leave it slightly ajar!), he bore her towards the bed, draped in luxurious rose-colored silk and heaped high with plump pillows.

"Goodnight, my love," he said, and deposited her on the bed —alone.

Green eyes flashed wickedly at her just before he nipped out the door, closing it behind him with decorous finality.

Amy gave a little wriggle of frustration. Drat the man—she'd almost had him!

Well, she'd be craftier next time. And there would certainly *be* a next time: she had several weeks left of summer to wear down his resistance! After all, even Thomas wasn't made of stone...

CHAPTER THREE

"Life is mostly froth and bubble,
Two things stand like stone,
KINDNESS in another's trouble,
COURAGE in your own."
—ADAM LINDSAY GORDON, "Ye Wearie Wayfarer"

TRUE TO HER RESOLVE, Amelia called upon the Livingstons the following morning. Thomas accompanied her, intrigued by what she'd told him about this family: prominent and populous, with an old name but an abundance of new wealth, which made them less likely to despise those with shorter pedigrees. And this particular branch of the clan had been consistently friendly to the Newbolds. According to Amelia, they'd also been among the first to welcome Aurelia back into Society after her accident.

Maritime, the Livingston "cottage,"—Thomas still couldn't quite wrap his mind about using this term to describe such an abode—was a handsome, well-proportioned house, though less grandiose than the Ogdens' new residence: more Italian villa than French château. There was an almost eerie sense of quiet here, though: Thomas noticed it the moment they were admitted, and to judge from the furrow that appeared between his fiancée's brows, he suspected she felt it too.

Not surprising, he supposed, given what this family was dealing with. He wondered if they would even agree to see Amelia and himself. But the butler who'd taken his fiancée's card soon returned to escort them upstairs to the family's private parlor. Mrs. Livingston was currently out, he informed them, but her two eldest daughters, Mrs. Reid—formerly Miss Venetia —and Miss Geneva, would be glad to receive them.

Thomas exchanged a quick glance with Amelia: if the girl who'd been kidnapped was willing to receive callers, surely that must be a good sign.

They were shown into an airy room decorated in soft pastels. Two young women sat side by side on a brocaded sofa; the taller of the two rose to her feet at once, smiling, as Thomas and Amelia entered.

"Dear Amy, so happy to see you again!" she exclaimed, coming forward with outstretched hands.

"Venetia, how lovely you look!"

The two women exchanged a quick kiss of greeting, then Amelia turned to Thomas. "And this is my fiancé, Thomas Sheridan. Thomas, Venetia Reid and her sister, Geneva Livingston."

Mrs. Reid extended her hand, which Thomas bowed over. "So, *you're* Amy's young man," she observed with a smile. "Delighted to meet you, Mr. Sheridan."

"The pleasure is mine, Mrs. Reid," Thomas assured her. "And Miss Livingston," he added, approaching the sofa with an outstretched hand.

She accepted it tentatively, with downcast eyes and a murmured greeting. Mindful of her discomfort, Thomas stepped back, returning to Amelia's side.

They were lovely young women, the Livingston sisters, he mused. Exactly the sort to delight a portrait painter: tall and slim, with dark hair and porcelain-fair complexions. Mrs. Reid was perhaps a fraction taller than her sister, with striking dark eyes and the vivacity so often noted in American ladies. By contrast, Miss Geneva was almost English in her reserve, but then that could be due to her recent ordeal. Perhaps she had been more like her older sister before her abduction? He would have to ask Amelia, when they were done calling.

Just then, a dainty King Charles spaniel emerged from beneath a chair and made straight for Geneva, sitting at her feet and gazing up at her with melting brown eyes. Geneva's face brightened, became genuinely animated, transforming its doll-like prettiness into something more human... and far more attractive. Leaning down, she scooped the dog into her arms, clearly undeterred by the prospect of paw prints and fur upon her pristine white day gown.

"Why, who is this?" Amelia exclaimed, smiling.

"This is Clementine." Geneva stroked the spaniel's glossy coat. "Clemmie for short."

"She's just darling," Amelia said, reaching out to let the dog sniff her fingers.

"She was a present for my eighteenth birthday, and she goes just about everywhere with me," Geneva added, with a smile that made her deep blue eyes glow.

Lady with a Dog, Thomas's imagination supplied. He wondered idly if the Livingstons had considered having Miss Geneva's portrait painted: walking her spaniel, perhaps. Unless, he remembered uncomfortably, her experience made her averse to such outings.

"Has she taken to Newport?" Amelia asked. "There must be tons of things for her to see—and smell on your walks together!"

Geneva's smile dimmed just a little. "I think she likes it here. Though we don't walk very far—just around the garden."

Mrs. Reid glanced anxiously at her sister before entering the conversation. "We've been leading rather a quiet life this summer, Amy." She paused, then resumed with the directness Thomas found characteristic of so many Americans, "I am not sure you'll have heard, but—"

"If you're referring to what happened to your sister last winter, then, yes, I have," Amelia replied with equal frankness. "Mrs. Ogden told us about the kidnappings when we attended her dinner party last night. It wasn't gossip," she added hastily, "Mother wanted to know if your family had come to Newport, that's all! And I am so sorry, Geneva, that you should have experienced such a terrible ordeal, and I hope you're doing better now."

Geneva flushed, but summoned a tiny smile, for friendship's sake if nothing else, Thomas suspected. "Thank you, Amy—that's very kind of you. I have been doing a *little* better this past month or so. Getting away from the city helped."

"Of course it must," Amelia said swiftly, "and I can certainly understand why you wouldn't want to accept many invitations at present. But I do hope you and your family will consider attending my engagement ball at Shore House, in two weeks' time."

"Why, how lovely!" Mrs. Reid exclaimed. "Jenny, dear, you must admit it sounds perfectly lovely," she added to her sister, whose flush deepened. "And the Newbolds have always been such good friends to us."

"And we count you among our closest friends too," Amelia chimed in. "But, truly, I don't wish to press you for an answer just now. Please take all the time you need to decide—the invitations haven't even been officially sent out yet."

"Thank you," Geneva said again, with almost palpable gratitude. Her eyes looked a touch wistful, Thomas thought. "I appreciate your thoughtfulness, and Venetia is right: it does sound lovely. And Shore House is such a charming place. I will—let you know as soon as possible," she finished, all in a rush. As if sensing her distress, her little spaniel licked her hand.

Amelia smiled at her friend. "That's all anyone can ask of you. Now, do tell us more about your delightful Clemmie."

"THERE's something about Geneva that reminds me a little of Relia," Amelia confessed to Thomas as they descended the stairs some minutes later. "She withdrew into herself too, after her accident. It took so long for her to try to reclaim herself. I hate seeing someone else suffer like that as well—and for something that wasn't even her fault."

"Do you think she'll attend?" Thomas asked.

"I hope so. I think perhaps, deep down, she would *like* to. In any case, I'm going to suggest to Mother that we have several corners where our guests can just sit quietly without being disturbed. And perhaps," her face took on a contemplative look, "perhaps we might even set up a pen for Geneva's puppy. She did say Clemmie goes everywhere with her—and she seems very well behaved. Clemmie, I mean. Geneva's deportment goes without saying."

Thomas shook his head, smiling. "Only you, sweetheart, would think to include a puppy in your invitation!"

Her eyes danced, but her reply was perfectly serious. "Well, why not? I can think of several *people* whose manners aren't as good as Clemmie's. And if having her puppy with her makes Geneva feel more comfortable..." She broke off, peering at him uncertainly. "What *are* you thinking, Thomas? I don't recall seeing that expression before."

He took her hand, lacing their fingers together, as they stepped through the door the Livingstons' butler held open for them. "I'm thinking that your friends are very fortunate to have you in their corner. Though not as fortunate as I am," he added, and saw her blush delightfully.

"Amy? Amy Newbold?" an unfamiliar male voice exclaimed.

A young man was coming up the walk: a tall, handsome young man of perhaps twenty-five, with dark hair, wearing immaculate tennis whites. Thomas thought he detected a decided resemblance to the two ladies they'd just visited, a suspicion confirmed by Amelia's next words.

"Larry Livingston!" she greeted the new arrival brightly. "How nice to see you again."

"The pleasure is mine," Livingston assured her, coming to a halt before them. "You're prettier than ever, if that's even possible."

She smiled. "Thank you. Larry, this is Thomas Sheridan, my

fiancé. Thomas, this is Larry Livingston, Venetia and Geneva's older brother."

Thomas extended his hand. "How do you do, Mr. Livingston?"

The moment the words were out, he saw a change come over the young man's face—a slight cooling of the sort he'd seen from several American men he'd met since coming here.

"Mr. Sheridan." Livingston returned a perfunctory handshake. "English, are you?"

"Indeed," Thomas said mildly. He was aware of the faint, puzzled frown creasing Amelia's brow. Astute as she was, she'd doubtless picked up the nuances of this exchange, but not the reason for it.

"Thomas is a noted artist, Larry," she said, her tone slightly rebuking. "He exhibited at the Royal Academy this past spring. His portrait of the Lady of Shalott was much praised."

She'd mentioned his painting instead of his pedigree: God, how he loved this woman. Much to his surprise, he saw Livingston unbend just a trifle.

"Congratulations, Mr. Sheridan." There was a grudging note of respect in his voice. "I understand that's quite an achievement."

"Thank you, Mr. Livingston," Thomas returned as pleasantly as if he hadn't noticed the younger man's previous hostility. "I felt very honored to be chosen by the committee."

"Thomas and I called upon your sisters, to extend an invitation to our engagement ball two weeks from now," Amelia continued.

"Ah." Livingston's expression altered yet again, concern lending a much more amiable cast to his features. "Amy, I don't know if you've heard—"

"About Geneva?" she finished for him. "As a matter of fact, I have, and I'm so sorry she experienced something so terrible. And very glad that she seems to be recovering. I've told her to take all the time she needs before responding, though I hope to see her and the rest of your family in attendance."

Livingston relaxed visibly. "Thank you—for your concern

and for the invitation. We've all been worried about Jenny. Hopefully, a change of scene and a spell of country living will perk her up." His face darkened, and his grip tightened around his tennis racket. "God knows *she* did nothing wrong, and I'd like to get my hands on the fellows who did this to her!"

"Perhaps the police will finally turn up something," Amelia suggested.

"That's what we're hoping." Livingston glanced at his watch. "Excuse me, but I have to go up and change, or I'll be late for luncheon. A pleasure meeting you both."

~

"I DON'T KNOW what the matter is with Larry," Amy remarked as they climbed into the Newbold carriage. "His manners are usually impeccable, but just now he seemed almost… rude."

Thomas shrugged. "Actually, compared to some of your countrymen, Mr. Livingston was almost cordial."

"Someone else has been rude to you? Who?" she demanded at once.

"Sweetheart, I'd prefer not to tell tales out of school—"

"Piffle!" Amy interrupted heatedly. "I won't have my future husband—the man I love—slighted by people who aren't fit to shine his shoes, no matter how much money they have!"

He looked simultaneously amused and touched by her partisanship. "Well, you need not take up the cudgels in my defense, my dear. The English know how to deal with such minor irritants, mainly by refusing even to acknowledge them. Besides, I suspect I know the root of your compatriots' hostility."

Amy raised inquiring brows.

"Another penniless English aristo carrying off one of *their* young women—one of their princesses, in fact. I can sympathize to some degree; their loss is unquestionably my gain."

"Well, you're not exactly penniless and I happen to know that you're not marrying me for my money. I'm the one who proposed, remember?" she pointed out.

A corner of his mouth crooked up. "One of my most cherished memories."

"And mine." Amy wove her fingers through his, leaning back against the carriage seat and mulling over what he'd told her. She suspected that she knew the identity of at least one of those men, even if Thomas refused to name names. "Well, it's ridiculous of them to resent you on that account. If Larry or... any *other* man of our set were interested in me, they should have spoken up a long time ago! So it's just too silly for words that they resent you or anyone else for taking an American bride!"

"I admit to some surprise at the degree of their resentment," he confessed. "I thought most American men were wealthy enough to pick and choose when it came to marriage."

"Well, the *older* men are," she explained. "They're the ones holding the purse strings, after all. But their sons are a different matter: they may get a handsome allowance, but not unlimited access to their fathers' money. *And* they're still expected to make something of themselves. Look at Andrew." Her older brother was putting in regular hours at the Newbold shipping offices and had voluntarily chosen to remain in New York for the present and work, instead of accompanying them to Newport.

"I suspect not every young man of your set's as diligent as Andrew, however."

"No, and more's the pity," she agreed. "Some are thoroughly spoiled, and shiftless as well. I'm sure they'd much rather marry a fortune than work for one or wait to inherit their father's. Fortunately, most girls I know have too much sense to accept an offer from them. Venetia had to turn Theo Van Horn down three times before he finally got the message—and two of his proposals were made *after* John Reid started courting her."

She saw the flicker of recognition in his eyes at the name. *Aha.* One mystery solved. Theo Van Horn—a college friend of Tony Ogden's and one particularly conceited New York scion—had been among the guests at The Cliffs last night. Amy could easily imagine him trying to snub Thomas.

"Of course, I imagine resentments against Englishmen may run higher just now because some of the old Knickerbocker families aren't doing so well these days," she went on. "The Van Horns had to dismiss half of their staff, I've heard. And the Schuylers didn't come to Newport at all this summer, on account of the expense."

"The Schuylers?"

"They made their fortune in real estate a good thirty years ago, but I gather their firm has been in a slump lately. Fortunately for them, Edith—their eldest daughter—got married last autumn, and their next girl won't be out for a while, so they can forego the Season this year. That's their cottage coming up right there," Amy pointed to the turreted mansion on the left. "The Sands. Strange to think of it all boarded up for the summer."

"Pity they didn't rent it out instead," Thomas observed, surveying the house in turn.

"And proclaim their straitened circumstances to the world? Heaven forbid!"

"I see your point—appearances must be kept up. In which respect, the English and Americans are remarkably similar."

"Then we might end up understanding each other, after all!" she laughed.

"Perhaps. 'We really have everything in common with America nowadays, except, of course, language,'" Thomas quoted.

Amy frowned consideringly. "Is that from Oscar Wilde?"

"Yes—very good. 'The Canterville Ghost.' And he has a definite point, because I doubt I will ever get used to hearing a mansion referred to as 'a cottage' or Newport as 'country living.' *English* country life generally means something more literal: trees, moors, fields... terrorizing the local game birds."

Amy shuddered. "You English are so bloodthirsty!"

His green eyes crinkled. "Acquit me of that, sweetheart. I'd much rather paint the native fauna than shoot it. And don't deny you Americans engage in blood sports as well."

"You mean, duck shooting? Or husband-hunting?" she inquired with limpid innocence, and had the reward of hearing him laugh outright. "Well, you don't have to worry on either score! The former doesn't take place until autumn, and as for the latter—"

"I surrendered willingly," he finished. "Without firing a single shot, as I recall."

"Your recall is perfect." Amy rested her head against his shoulder. "Now, if you would prefer to engage in Newport pastimes of a less violent nature, I can suggest yachting, tennis, promenading, gambling, shopping—"

He pulled a face. "It all sounds very fatiguing."

"It can be, to someone who's not used to it. Although I've just thought of something you might find exhilarating rather than exhausting." At his look of inquiry, she glanced up at the cloudless summer sky, which promised more heat as the day wore on. "How would you enjoy a swim, Mr. Sheridan?"

LIKE MANY COTTAGERS, the Newbolds had purchased one of the private bathhouses in the elegant new pavilion—built last year to replace the decrepit bathing huts on Bailey's Beach, Amy informed her fiancé. They ducked inside to change, though Thomas was ready first, his brows rising towards his hairline when Amy emerged in the appropriate costume.

"It must be love," he observed. "That I can find you beautiful even in something as hideous as that bathing dress."

Amy wrinkled her nose as she contemplated her navy-blue tunic and bloomers. "It is rather awful, isn't it?"

He cast his gaze heavenward. "My dear girl, it resembles all the sailor suits inflicted on countless small boys—and I include myself—unable to defend themselves against such a sartorial offense!"

"Well, it's the current fashion for swimming, and believe me, there were others I *didn't* purchase that were much worse!" she pointed out. Thomas, of course, looked good enough to eat in a close-fitting bathing suit of black wool that flattered his lean figure. Not for the first time, Amy reflected that men enjoyed a distinct advantage when it came to sporting wear.

He crossed his arms, assuming a long-suffering expression that made her want to giggle. "What other strange native custom must we next observe, sweetheart?"

"Well," Amy began, "we could proceed down to the water, where we may bob up and down in the shallows for the next hour or so, in the abundant company of people we will come to know far too well this summer. Or…" she lowered her lashes demurely, "we could slip away to somewhere more private and actually *enjoy* the beach."

"I vote for the second," he said at once.

"An excellent choice, sir," she approved. "If we head further east, the beach is usually not so crowded. At least, it's less likely that we'll encounter any 'cottagers' there." *And we'll be together, with fewer prying eyes upon us.*

After a quick glance around to make certain they were unobserved, Amy led the way towards the east end of the beach. As she had foreseen, there were only a handful of bathers and waders present, all too occupied with their own amusement to spare her and Thomas more than a perfunctory glance.

"Much better," her fiancé remarked, surveying the scene with approval.

"Relia and I used to slip away like this, when we wanted some privacy," Amy told him as they headed towards the water. "Time simply to be sisters and friends, without the rest of Newport looking on or wanting to know our business."

"Understandable—you and Aurelia have always seemed particularly close."

"And this was one of our favorite spots, though I suspect the beach at Trevenan has since replaced Bailey's in her affections."

Smiling, Thomas reached for her hand. "Then I'm doubly honored that you're sharing it with me now. Shall we walk?"

Beneath the afternoon sun, the sea glowed like liquid sapphires, and the sand—while rockier than was ideal—was soft enough underfoot at the water's edge. Amy curled her bare toes as the water, deliciously cold, lapped about her ankles. Thomas too began to relax under the soothing influences of sea, sun, and relative solitude. Imagining ways to capture the scene in oils or watercolors, she suspected.

No need for conversation when they were so in harmony, with nature and each other, Amy reflected contentedly. Instead, they strolled along the strip of beach for a while, then, as one, sat down on the sand, just out of reach of the tide.

He kissed her then, and she could taste the faint tang of salt on his lips, brought there by the brisk sea wind. She kissed him back with equal enthusiasm, relishing the rare freedom they now shared: just a man and a woman beneath the midday sun, the tumbling sea at their feet.

More kisses followed, and he drew her to him, his long artist's fingers toying with the hair she'd woven into one long plait. "I should paint you like this," he murmured against her mouth. "But without the bathing dress, only your hair loose and flowing down to cover you."

"Like a mermaid's?"

"A sea nymph's," he corrected. "No fishtail to contend with, just those long, slim legs…"

His green eyes had gone soft and dreamy, but she could see the heat in them too, smoldering like a barely banked fire. Victory beckoned, and she laid her hand upon his chest, felt the strong beat of his heart under her palm. He stilled beneath her touch, hardly seeming to breathe.

"Thoooomassss," she crooned, trailing her hand down towards his abdomen—and below. "You *know* you want me. I can tell." Her gaze lingered on a part of his body that, in the last few minutes, had become increasingly visible through his bathing suit.

"Ah. Most inconvenient." Did he sound a little breathless? "I cannot deny the truth of your words, sweetheart. Fortunately, I believe I know the perfect remedy." He stood up, pulling her to her feet.

"Thomas, what are you—?"

The rest of the question was lost in a shriek as he tossed her over his shoulder, then ran down the beach and plunged into the nearest wave.

CHAPTER FOUR

Art is a jealous mistress.
—Ralph Waldo Emerson, *The Conduct of Life*

Two weeks later

Rather than try to compete with grander homes like The Cliffs or Château-sur-Mer, Laura Newbold had decided to let Shore House's charms speak for themselves. Not ornate or ostentatious, but rather elegant, subtle, and refined. Amy had wholeheartedly agreed with her mother's vision and together, they'd worked tirelessly for the last two weeks to bring it about.

Their efforts had paid off handsomely: by the night of the ball, Shore House was immaculate, all its woodwork polished to a high gloss. Every prism in the crystal chandelier sparkled like a diamond of the first water, and the French doors of the Grand Salon stood open to the garden, which was Laura's particular pride and joy.

Even by moonlight, the sight of the flowerbeds in bloom took one's breath away. Colored paper lanterns illuminated the hydrangea bushes, heavy with clusters of white and brilliant blue blossoms. The mingled scents of jasmine, honeysuckle, and rose drifted inside, an intoxicating bouquet, while more flowers —in bright, summery hues—adorned the ballroom, draped with swaths of white and deep blue silk.

Nearly all of Newport must be here tonight, Amy mused as she watched the steady influx of guests into the salon. Some with whom she could have happily dispensed, like Theo Van Horn. But one couldn't exclude a guest merely because one suspected him of rudeness—Thomas still refused to identify those who had tried to snub him—and the Van Horns as a family were largely unobjectionable, if a bit stodgy and self-important. But their social prominence in New York was such that Amy's mother would have felt acutely uncomfortable about excluding them.

And then there were the Vandermeres, who'd been invited for a similar reason *and* to show that the Newbolds were willing to let bygones be bygones... especially in light of Relia's wedded bliss, Amy reflected with satisfaction. Indeed, to judge from her twin's most recent letter, Relia was ecstatically happy in her marriage, with not a thought to spare for Stupid Charlie! *He* was still absent from Newport—only his parents and Sally had come tonight, and Amy supposed she could exert herself to be cordial to them, if necessary.

She was far more pleased when the Livingstons arrived—all but their two youngest children who were not yet out. But Larry, Venetia, Mark, and Geneva entered in their parents' wake, along with Venetia's husband. Laura Newbold, all smiles, greeted the family warmly as they approached, and she and Mrs. Livingston were soon chatting comfortably, with the ease of old friends.

"Geneva!" Amy held out welcoming hands to the girl. "I'm so happy that you came."

Geneva mustered a shy smile but clasped her hands in return. "I'm—happy to *be* here, Amy. And thank you for including Clemmie in the invitation, but I do think I might be able to get by without her, for one evening. Shore House looks beautiful tonight, by the way," she added, glancing about the ballroom.

Amy smiled. "Thank you. We believe that Mama has outdone herself for the occasion."

"I like the blue and white. It's as if the sea and the sky have been brought inside."

"Yes, that's it exactly," Amy said, pleased. "Mama wanted our guests to feel as cool and comfortable indoors as they would outdoors. Not an easy task, on a summer night with so many people present!"

And it seemed to be working. Amy noticed that quite a number of guests seemed to relax visibly as soon as they set foot inside the ballroom. Beautiful surroundings could make all the difference, she decided.

"Well, it looks lovely, and so do you, in that gown," Geneva said admiringly. "Is it Worth?"

"But of course! I would hardly dare to wear anyone else for such an occasion." The rich ivory satin, with its shell-pink embellishments, was a shade or two darker than the wedding gown Amy would be donning in barely three months' time, but almost as elaborate. "And you look lovely too—that shade of blue is perfect for your coloring."

And the flush of pink in Geneva's cheeks was even more becoming, she thought. The girl looked—a little tentative, perhaps, but not nervous or anxious. Amy hoped that boded well for her enjoyment of the evening.

"By the way," she added as casually as possible, "we just planted a new species of night-blooming orchid in our conservatory. For the added enjoyment of our guests."

Geneva's eyes widened in comprehension—and gratitude. The conservatory, with its soft lighting and wicker furniture, was one of the most tranquil rooms in Shore House: an ideal refuge for guests seeking temporary escape from a crowded ballroom.

"Thank you," she replied, after a moment. "That sounds very pleasant. I'll be sure to visit the conservatory this evening, to see it."

They exchanged a quick smile of understanding, then Geneva and the other Livingstons proceeded further into the ballroom, as the Russells—also friends of the family —approached.

"Deftly done, sweetheart," a familiar voice remarked from behind her.

Amy started, then relaxed. "Thomas!" she chided. "You made me jump—am I going to have to put a bell on you?"

"Will it start a new fashion if you do?" he inquired with genuine interest.

"In Newport? All too likely. On second thought," she subjected him to a lingering, head-to-toe scrutiny, "you look quite handsome without one."

Handsome—and to her secret relief, less... distracted than he'd sometimes appeared of late, when she'd had to leave him more to his own devices as the date of the party neared. Ordinarily, that wouldn't have been a problem: much as they enjoyed each other's company, they both understood that they did not need to spend *every* waking moment together, and Amy knew how essential privacy was to Thomas when he was working. He'd already produced watercolors of the beach and the Cliff Walk, as well as a series of very fine sketches in charcoal of a clambake they'd attended.

This past week, however, she'd sensed a certain restlessness about him. And experienced the growing conviction that his mind was elsewhere, though he was as affectionate as ever when they were alone together. Which relieved her mind of niggling doubts that he might be regretting their engagement —mostly.

Nonetheless, something wasn't wholly right with him. Could it be homesickness? It wasn't easy to immerse oneself wholly in the culture and customs of another country, even if one spoke the language. Amy herself had been a little daunted when she first set foot on English soil, and poor Relia—still suffering from the lingering effects of her accident—had hardly dared to venture out of their suite at Claridge's. Here in Newport, surrounded by curious and occasionally overfamiliar Americans, it was not inconceivable that Thomas might be missing England.

All the more reason to appreciate his presence at her side tonight. She smiled brilliantly at him, and saw an answering smile warm his eyes, dispelling some of her anxiety. Later, perhaps, when they were alone, she could ask him about what might be troubling him.

"Do you know, sweetheart, this may be the most English party I've attended in America," he observed now, scanning the ballroom and the assembled guests.

"Is that a compliment?" Amy inquired, having heard his trenchant observations about certain English entertainments.

"In this case, yes. It reminds me of some of my mother's parties—in the best possible way, I assure you. Elegant, *au courant*, and just lavish enough."

And as Lady Julia Sheridan was accounted an excellent hostess, Amy let herself relax. "I'll be sure to tell Mama that. She's been quite anxious about everything being just right this evening."

His hand came to rest on the small of her back, a caress that was light, intimate, and familiar at once. "With all due respect for your mother's efforts, the only thing required for perfection tonight is the two of us—together."

She leaned into his touch. "Then we're in perfect accord, Mr. Sheridan, as always."

THE BALL officially began at ten o'clock, and Amy and Thomas played their parts as expected, opening the dancing with a quadrille. The official announcement of their betrothal—an hour or so into the festivities—was only a formality, but it was pleasant to receive the congratulations and good wishes of people Amy had known for much of her life.

The guests also appeared to be enjoying themselves—including Geneva, Amy was pleased to note. Although the girl seemed disposed to linger in the quieter corners of the ballroom,

Amy did glimpse her engaging in a few dances as well; Andrew, who'd come down from New York for the party, partnered her in one of the slower waltzes.

For her part, Amy found herself fairly danced off her feet. Not that she minded, as Thomas was her most frequent partner, but it was a relief to discover that she'd left a Lancers unclaimed, so she could enjoy a short respite. Slipping into a secluded alcove with Thomas, she fanned herself vigorously, certain that her face was the shade of a well-boiled lobster.

Thomas leaned against the alcove wall. "Shall I procure us some refreshment?" he asked, looking as fresh as he had when the evening began—which was almost unforgivable of him.

"That would be wonderful!" Amy declared fervently, tucking a stray curl behind her ear.

"Anything my lady particularly desires?"

"An ice, please—if there are any left." To judge from the number of people she'd seen consuming them, they'd proven to be especially popular. "Any flavor will do, though raspberry's my favorite."

"So I've observed. Your wish is my command." He sketched her a bow before departing.

Alone, Amy plied her fan and gazed out at the assembled couples on the dance floor. She caught sight of Geneva moving through the set, even smiling now and then at her brother-in-law, who was partnering her. No sign of disquiet or anxiety—so much the better. Indeed, all the guests Amy could see appeared to be fully enjoying themselves. The party was proving to be an unqualified success, of which any hostess might be justly proud. Indeed, every time Amy had seen her mother this evening, Laura Newbold had been flushed with triumph and pleasure.

Intent on the dancers, Amy was barely aware of someone slipping into the alcove behind her—another woman, to judge from the accompanying rustle of skirts. Automatically, she moved aside to make room.

The newcomer murmured almost inaudible thanks, then said more clearly—if still tentatively, "Good evening, Amy."

Amy stiffened, immediately recognizing the voice. But she

45

maintained an expression of distant courtesy as she turned around. "Good evening, Sally. I hope that you're enjoying yourself this evening."

"Oh, yes. This is a wonderful party, Amy," Sally Vandermere ventured, her expression almost... timid. "And I was very happy to be invited."

"We are—pleased that you and your family could attend," Amy replied, hoping that a bolt of lightning would *not* strike her down for the polite untruth.

"Charlie couldn't—but then he's been far too busy in the city to come down to Newport this summer."

Amy managed a sweetly insincere smile at the news. "What a pity."

Flushing, Sally bit her lip. "Amy, I hope you won't take offense at this, but... I'd like to clear the air between us." She took a breath, then rushed on, "I know that you and the rest of your family don't much like Charlie after the way he treated Aurelia—and I can't say that I blame you," she added hurriedly. "I'd feel exactly the same in your place. Just—well, I want you to know that *I* personally would have been glad to have Aurelia for a sister."

Amy stared at her. This must be the first time *any* Vandermere had admitted fault in their treatment of her twin. Perhaps, she reflected a little guiltily, she had been less than fair to Sally, who had—after all—been much too young to have had any involvement in her brother's heartless jilting of the girl who loved him. Certainly *she* wasn't to blame for Stupid Charlie being... well, stupid.

"Anyway, I hope your sister is very happy in her marriage," Sally continued. "She deserves to be. I thought Lord Trevenan seemed very pleasant, from what I saw of him."

Amy allowed herself to thaw a little further. "Relia is very happy, Sally—thank you for inquiring. And Lord Trevenan is the most estimable of men." She should know, having been briefly engaged to him herself. "He and my sister are ideally suited to one another," she added. "Just as Mr. Sheridan and I are."

Sally nodded, looking slightly wistful. "How romantic that

you and Aurelia should have found your perfect matches this year! I hope *I* can be as lucky someday."

"Has anyone taken your fancy yet?" Amy inquired, more from a wish to be pleasant than from any real curiosity. But if Sally could make the effort, then so could she.

"Well, I've only just come out this year, so I haven't really settled on any one person," the girl confessed. "Although…" she glanced over her shoulder, then pointed mischievously with her fan, "there are two fellows who've been *very* attentive lately!"

Following her gesture, Amy saw Theo Van Horn and Tony Ogden approaching the alcove, each sporting a determined expression.

"I happened to mention that my next waltz was unclaimed— and I suspect they're both about to ask for it," Sally confessed, stifling a giggle. "I don't know whether I prefer Theo or Tony, but having them courting me this summer *has* been fun! Aren't they a handsome pair?"

Handsome is as handsome does. Amy bit back the tart observation in favor of a noncommittal "Mm." They were good-looking enough, she supposed, and both of a similar physical type: blond and athletic, even a little beefy. A matched set… *like Tweedledee and Tweedledum*, a voice in her head—that sounded very like Thomas—remarked sardonically. She wondered if Sally knew about the Van Horns' recent financial difficulties and whether she should mention them. But she couldn't think of a way to do so without sounding spiteful or catty, as though she were trying to spoil a young girl's innocent pleasure in her beaux. Nor did she wish to stay and exchange pleasantries with a man she suspected of discourtesy towards her fiancé.

Fortunately, at that moment she spied Thomas, approaching with a crystal bowl—heaped high with the requested ices—in each hand.

"Ah, there's Thomas," she reported brightly. "Please excuse me, Sally. I hope you enjoy the rest of the evening."

Slipping out of the alcove, she went to meet him. He handed her one of the bowls with a flourish. "Raspberry ice, as my lady requested."

47

"Thank you, sir!" Amy dipped her spoon into the ice-pink confection, savored the sweet coldness on her tongue. "Um, delicious!"

He sampled his own—lemon, pale and icy—and nodded in approval. "As good as Gunter's, if not better. I hope I didn't keep you waiting too long."

"Not at all. I was just exchanging pleasantries—with Sally Vandermere, of all people."

His brows rose sharply. "*That* must have been an interesting conversation! No blood was shed, I trust?"

"Not a drop. Though that might not have been the case if Stupid Charlie had been present. Still," she conceded, "Sally's not to blame for *his* mistakes. I may not care much for the Vandermeres as a family, but I'll make an effort in future to treat each one as an individual, rather than tar them all with one brush!"

"A commendable resolution," Thomas remarked.

"And just one of many, I'll have you know."

"Oh? Pray continue, sweetheart."

"Well, my second resolution is to find a quiet corner, just for us, so we can enjoy these delicious ices. And my third," she smiled into his eyes, "is to dance until dawn—with you."

DAWN WAS INDEED SHOWING its face by the time the party ended. Too tired to steal more than a few kisses from her fiancé, Amy tumbled into bed as soon as she was undressed and slept dreamlessly.

She awoke when the sun was climbing towards midday, and enjoyed a light breakfast in her room. Inquiring about the rest of the family, she learned that her mother was still abed but her father and brother had both gone for a swim at Bailey's Beach. Mr. Sheridan, Mariette informed her, was up and working in the small parlor he liked to use as a studio.

Amy eagerly donned a pretty blue morning dress and went to join him. Pausing in the open doorway, she drank in the sight of Thomas standing before an easel, hard at work at what appeared to be a watercolor sketch of the Cliff Walk and some of the surrounding cottages.

There was an undeniable thrill, she decided, in watching one's lover do what he was meant to do. The light from the window limned Thomas in gold as if he were a painting himself. She could see his brows knit in a frown of concentration, his hair tousled and spilling over his high forehead, as his hand moved the brush over the page with almost surgical precision, applying daubs of blue and white to evoke a summer sky ornamented with puffball clouds.

He stepped back suddenly, the crease between his brows deepening as he studied his work in silence. Then, to Amy's shock, he reached out and slashed his brush in a large "X" across the paper. Once, and again, more violently—as though the painting had somehow offended him.

A sound of dismay escaped her, and Thomas glanced towards the doorway, his expression becoming almost embarrassed as he registered her presence.

"Thomas, what's wrong?" she asked, coming further into the room.

He blew out a breath, set down his brush, and offered her a wry smile. "An artistic tantrum. Sorry, sweetheart."

"There's no need to apologize." Amy assured him. She'd destroyed most of her own sketches and paintings once she'd discovered the limitations of her artistic ability. Crossing over to the easel, she studied the rejected painting. "What do you think is wrong with it?"

"Can't you see it?"

One more thing she loved about him: that he expected an honest opinion from her when it came to his work. And she would not disappoint him in that. Lips pursed, she examined the watercolor more closely—even critically.

"Well," she ventured, after a moment, "it looks *technically* proficient to me. And it's certainly not terrible. I can think of several people who'd be quite happy to have something like this hanging in their sitting room…"

"But?" he prompted, his gaze intent on her face.

Amy fidgeted beneath his scrutiny. "Bear in mind, Thomas, that this is still miles better than anything *I* could produce. But it seems a little… quieter than your usual style of work."

"You mean 'dull.'"

"I didn't say that!"

"You didn't have to. Nor have you seen the work I've already destroyed." He raked a hand through his hair. "Everything I've produced this past week has been like that: pretty, placid—and soulless."

"I think you're being much too hard on yourself," she said staunchly. "You've done some lovely work in Newport."

"A few pieces," he conceded. "But most of what I've done here feels… uninspired. As if the life—the vital pulse—is missing, in spite of how beautiful this place is." Grimacing, he dropped down onto the nearest chair, one hand shielding his eyes. "*All is silver-grey / Placid and perfect with my art: the worse!*"

Browning, Amy's memory supplied: one of his favorite poets —and hers. About Andrea Del Sarto, the "faultless painter" who might have aspired to more, had he not been in thrall to a demanding and covetous wife…

She bit her lip, struck by an idea to which she was reluctant to give voice. But this work was a vital part of the man she loved, and she would not be selfish. "Would—would a change of scene help?"

"Another region of Newport, you mean?"

"No, a more comprehensive change than that." She took a bracing breath. "You weren't uninspired when we first arrived in America. In fact, you said you could have painted all day and night, when we were in New York. Perhaps it would help, if you went back there for a while? Andrew and Father are both planning to depart tomorrow—you could go with them."

He looked up at that. "I don't want to leave *you*, Amelia."

The admission warmed her through and through; she found it easier to continue. "You wouldn't be. Not really. Lots of husbands and fathers spend the weekdays in the city, then come down for the weekend. And you've been here every day for the last two weeks, doing everything—well, *almost* everything—I want." Her maiden virtue was still intact, alas, despite her best efforts.

She saw the conflict in his eyes, the reluctance mingling with longing, and pressed on. "Thomas, if I had even a scintilla of your talent, I'd guard my time like a dragon guarding its hoard! How could I be so selfish as to begrudge you the time you need for your art?" She went to him, kneeling to frame his dearly loved face with her hands. "Go to New York, my dear—and come back with a masterpiece. I'll still be here, waiting."

He caught her to him, kissed her swiftly and fiercely. "There's not a woman in a thousand who would understand. Thank you for being that woman."

The sweetness of his praise alleviated the pang of their imminent parting. Who needed a sonnet composed to her eyebrow when the man she loved could summon eloquence like that? Locking her arms about his neck, she returned kiss for kiss.

"A masterpiece, mind," she murmured against his lips. "*And letters telling me about everything you find to paint in the city.*" Then, more softly, remembering Del Sarto's last words in the poem, "*Go, my Love.*"

CHAPTER FIVE

Then wilt thou speak of banqueting delights,
Of masks and revels which sweet youth did make.
—THOMAS CAMPION, *A Book of Airs*

NEW YORK, *31 August 1891*

MY DEAREST AMELIA—

By now I have settled in with your father and brother in the Fifth
Avenue house, where the three of us come and go according to our
varied schedules. In some respects, this reminds me of my earliest days
as an artist—long before you and even before my studio on Half Moon
Street—when I had rooms at the Albany and worked all manner of
strange hours. This return to semi-bachelorhood feels strange and not
wholly comfortable now, which I attribute entirely to your influence. A
disconcerting realization, but one that seems to bode well for our future
life together—would you not agree, sweetheart?

Nonetheless, I cannot deny that, as you suggested, New York has
proven to be a tonic as far as my work is concerned. During the day I
venture out with my sketchbook to explore parts of the city. Hardly an
hour passes when I do not see something worth capturing on paper,

*whether it's the sun rising over New York harbor, children playing in
Central Park, or the vendors hawking their wares on the Lower East
Side. I cannot promise a masterpiece as yet, but I believe I have
produced some worthwhile drawings that may perhaps yield to more.*

*Today, intrigued by the similarity of the name, I ventured into the
area your country calls Soho, where I spent most of the day trying to
capture the varied character of the place: from the theatres to the shops,
to the grand hotels and the somewhat—shall we say, less respectable
venues? Tomorrow, I plan to board the ferry to Coney Island for a
closer look at the Elephantine Colossus you pointed out to me from the
ship rail when we first entered the harbor. My one regret is that you
are not with me...*

~

NEWPORT, *3 September 1891*

"How long will Mr. Sheridan be gone?" Geneva asked as she
and Amy strolled through the garden at Shore House. Clemmie
trotted a little before them and sniffed at everything that caught
her interest, though her mistress kept a firm hold of her leash.

"Perhaps a week," Amy replied, with a resolute smile. "Certainly no more than two weeks. He's promised to be back by the
15th, when we'll be celebrating Mama's birthday. And he said
he'd write regularly. I just received his first letter today."

"The two of you seem so happy together," Geneva observed, a
bit wistfully. "You must miss him very much."

"I do," Amy confessed. "And I know he misses me as well. But
he is an artist, and if he feels stifled and unfulfilled here, then it's
only right that I let him go to a place where he can work. It's
only a temporary situation, after all." She changed the subject.
"Has anyone caught *your* fancy this summer, Geneva? I noticed
that several young men were very attentive to you at my engagement ball."

The younger girl turned slightly pink, but shook her head.
"Oh, no—I haven't got any beaux just yet. And if truth be told... I
don't feel ready for one. Especially not now," she added in a low
voice.

"Understood," Amy said lightly, knowing all too well the reason why. "No need to settle on anyone this soon. I was all of twenty-one when I succumbed to Thomas's charms."

"Twenty-one! A veritable old maid," Geneva teased gently.

"At my last prayers, as the English would say," Amy agreed.

They laughed and walked on together, breathing in the heady scent of roses mingled with bracing salt air. Off in the distance, the vast expanse of the sea shone like a mirror, reflecting back the deep blue of the sky. A perfect summer afternoon.

Geneva looked more relaxed than the last time Amy had seen her. And exceptionally pretty in a green and white ensemble that flattered her dark hair and fair complexion, with fresh color glowing in her cheeks. While she'd said she enjoyed Amy's engagement party, she still did not socialize often, so it had been a delightful surprise to receive a visit from her and Clemmie today, though Amy was careful not to make too much of it.

Reaching the gazebo in the middle of the garden, they climbed the steps and sat down together on one of the benches. Geneva scooped Clemmie onto her lap, cuddling the little spaniel close.

"Such a beautiful day," she said, gazing around them with apparent content. "I would dream about days like this last winter. About being here, near the sea. Everything seems so much more... manageable away from the city. Nothing to remind me of—what happened before."

"So you've been doing better, my dear?" Amy inquired solicitously.

Geneva nodded. "Mostly better. I've been trying to get out more. Yesterday, I went to the Casino. Venetia and I played tennis with John and Larry, and then we had tea. It was very pleasant. Tomorrow, if the weather continues fine, I may even go for a swim."

"I'm delighted that you've made such progress. Have you—felt up to attending evening entertainments too?"

"A few—we're to dine at the Russells' this Saturday. And I've heard there's to be music, afterwards: a violinist and then a noted soprano, who's apparently performed in Paris *and* Milan."

Geneva's eyes glowed with anticipation. "I *have* missed the opera, so I'm looking forward to that very much."

Amy smiled. "The Russells have invited us too, so we'll see you there. What about the Thurstons' masquerade next week? I've heard it's to be one of the highlights of the Season."

Some of the fresh color drained from Geneva's face. "I— don't think so," she demurred, lowering her gaze and fidgeting with Clemmie's collar. "I'm not really *comfortable*... with the idea of putting on a mask, or with being around people who are disguised. In fact—ever since it happened, I find myself growing anxious if I can't see someone's face clearly. If I can't recognize the people I'm with. You may think it strange—"

"Not at all!" Amy interrupted swiftly. "Forgive *me* for not realizing sooner. Were your abductors disguised?"

"I suppose they must have been. I never saw their faces." Geneva bit her lip. "Amy... how much did Mrs. Ogden tell you?"

"Not a great deal. Only that you—and the other two—were kidnapped while returning from social engagements." Amy paused, then resumed gently, "And you don't have to go into any more detail about it if it bothers you so."

Geneva shook her head almost vehemently. "Talking about my abduction isn't easy, but it's not nearly as awful as having experienced it! And my family believes..." she swallowed, then resumed more steadily, "my family believes that my speaking openly of it will give the whole ordeal less *power* over me. That it will make me less afraid. Less ashamed."

"You have *nothing* to be ashamed of!" Amy objected.

The younger girl blinked furiously. "That's what my family tells me too. But I can't help feeling that I was stupidly trusting and naïve. That I should have suspected something from the start." She paused, pressing the heels of her hands to her eyes. In her lap, Clemmie whimpered softly, sensing her mistress's distress.

"But how could you have?" Amy asked, bewildered.

"It was such... an unusual invitation. A little eccentric—but I told myself that even members of the Four Hundred have their idiosyncrasies. And it sounded like fun too, in a way."

PAMELA SHERWOOD

Geneva lowered her hands to caress her spaniel's silky head. "A Christmas party for puppies! Several of my friends were going. Mabel Ogden had a new Pekingese, and Edith Waddington—who was hosting it—had just acquired a pair of miniature poodles. So I took Clemmie, and there was this lovely supper for the dogs. Chopped chicken, shredded beef, even *pâté de foie gras*, though I didn't want Clemmie having too much of that. It might have made her ill. But she did seem to be enjoying herself with the other dogs, so I let it be.

"After a bit, I thought Clemmie had eaten enough, and it might be best to take her outside for—well, you know. So I put her on a leash and we went out into the garden. A footman offered me a cup of hot punch so I wouldn't freeze while I was out there.

"It was awfully sweet, but it was hot, so I drank it. But I felt so dizzy afterwards. I sat down on a bench, hoping it would help, and the next thing I knew there was a sack over my head!" Geneva shivered, her blue eyes going stark with remembered fear. "That's when they grabbed me, I tried to move, to fight, even to scream, but it was no good!

"And I heard Clemmie barking, trying to help me. Then I heard her cry out. One of those monsters must have kicked her! Venetia said they found her cowering in the bushes, after the kidnappers had taken me.

"I must have lost consciousness after that—I don't know whether it was the drug or the pure terror. When I came to, I was in this little room, all boarded up. No way to see out of the windows, and the doors were bolted. I was bound hand and foot, and gagged too—no way to scream, and I wonder if it would have done any good if I had. If anyone would have heard me."

"Were you left entirely alone?"

"Someone—it was so dark I couldn't tell if it was a man or a woman—came in with a tray. Just bread and water. And there was a chamber pot if I needed to use it. I was untied long enough for that, then bound again so I wouldn't get any ideas of trying to escape when my restraints were gone." Her mouth twisted.

56

"Not that I *could* have. I was so stiff by then that I could barely stand, much less run."

"Did your jailer say anything to you? Anything by which you might able to recognize him—or her?"

Geneva shook her head. "He—or she—was as silent as the grave. And I never heard my abductors talking among themselves either. I couldn't tell how long I was there—it felt like an eternity, but I learned afterwards that Papa had paid the ransom within two days. And then I was taken out the same way I'd been brought in, bound, gagged, and with a sack over my head. "I don't even know where they left me," she went on hurriedly. "Some spot agreed upon in the ransom note, I think. They set me down on the ground—it was so cold, I could feel it through my dress, and then they left. I heard them moving off—two sets of footsteps, maybe three. And then the next thing I know, Papa and Larry were there, taking off the sack and untying me." She paused, her lips crimping. "I started to cry when I saw them, and the doctor had to give me a sedative because I couldn't seem to stop."

Amy squeezed her hand in sympathy. "Oh, my dear!"

Geneva closed her eyes for a moment. "When I woke up, the police were there," she continued, her voice strained. "I told them everything I could remember, as I've just told you."

"Have they discovered anything?" Amy asked gently. "Anything at all?"

Geneva shook her head. "They investigated as thoroughly as they could, but found nothing. And the Waddingtons have apologized again and again—they still have no idea how the kidnappers managed to get in and out of their garden unnoticed. And then, after Maisie, the abductions just... stopped. Before we left for Newport, Papa asked the chief of police if there'd been any further developments, but after more than six months, the trail's gone cold."

Amy shivered. "No wonder you've been having such a hard time of it."

"I would give just about anything for it to be over—*somehow!*" Geneva's arms tightened about Clemmie, who whined softly and

57

tried to lick her mistress's face. "I want them caught as much as Papa does! I want to be able to go for a walk without feeling as though someone's following me. I want to be able to—to go to a concert or the theater and not see the pitying looks or hear the whispers." Her eyes filled. "My family says I've done nothing wrong. That I should remember I'm a Livingston of New York. That I should hold my head high and be the life and soul of every party I attend. Except that I *never* was like that, even before! Venetia was the outgoing one, and Florrie is going to be just like her! *I* was the 'quiet Livingston sister.' And now I have to pretend to be this—this social butterfly just to show the rest of the world that I'm not ruined or broken…"

She choked to a stop, covering her face with her hands. Clemmie whimpered in sympathy, and Amy put an arm about the younger girl.

"Of course you're not ruined, *or* broken!" she declared staunchly. "You've had a terrible experience, and you need time to recover—at your own pace and no one else's."

"Thank you," Geneva managed after a moment. "For understanding. I wish my family did." She pulled away and took out a handkerchief, blotting her eyes. "It's not that I want to be a recluse. Or a coward. But I can't pretend to be what I'm not, and I can't deny that some things still—frighten me. Like crowds. Or unfamiliar surroundings. And I can only bear going out at night if I'm with people I trust completely. Alice feels the same way."

"Alice Carr?"

Geneva nodded. "Maisie couldn't receive visitors, after, but Alice and I have spoken about what happened to us. Who else would understand?" A bleak smile ghosted about her mouth. "So we compared our 'war stories.' *She* was abducted about two weeks earlier from a skating party in Central Park. They grabbed her when she left the ice for a short rest, just the way they grabbed me—by coming up behind her and throwing a sack over her head."

"But didn't anyone else at the party notice that she was missing?"

"According to the police, her friends all thought she'd gone home early," Geneva replied. "And there must have been dozens of people on the ice that evening. It would have been easy to lose sight of one skater in a crowd."

"The kidnappers were probably counting on that," Amy observed grimly.

"The police thought so too. Poor Alice woke up the way I did: bound, gagged, and held in some dark little room with the windows boarded up. They didn't even take her skates off."

Which would have rendered Alice even more helpless, Amy thought. Something niggled at her mind: the abductors seemed to have some knowledge of their victims' habits—what they liked, where they went, who their friends were. That argued for a certain degree of... premeditation. Of course, the kidnappers could have been observing—and stalking their prey for weeks. The thought made her blood run cold.

"Alice's father paid the ransom even faster than Papa," Geneva went on. "Not that it helped. Alice told me she became a nervous wreck just walking down Fifth Avenue. That all the places she loved to go were tainted for her now. That's why she went abroad this summer—to get away from everything that reminded her of *it*." She took a shaky breath and cuddled Clemmie to her, letting the little spaniel lick her chin. "I hope she's doing better than I am!"

Amy laid a hand over hers. "*I* think you're doing just fine, my dear. And that you're so much braver than you realize."

Geneva managed a wobbly smile. "I don't *feel* very brave. But thank you all the same."

"Shall we go in now, and have some tea? I know it's not a panacea, but..."

"Tea would be lovely, Amy. Thank you again."

～

Newport, 9 September 1891

A clear, starry summer night, with just a breath of wind stirring the trees. Perfect for a masquerade, Amy thought as she followed her mother up the steps of the Thurstons' grand summer home, Château de Sable. Personally, Amy preferred the English term—Sandcastle—and if she and Thomas ever acquired their own cottage by the sea, she might suggest calling it that.

But the Thurstons had certainly decorated their home with a magnificence suited to its name and the occasion. Entering the ballroom, Amy found herself dazzled by the silk hangings in every shade of the rainbow, the arrangements of massed summer flowers, and the fully illuminated crystal chandelier ablaze in the center of the ceiling.

At least she and her mother were gowned with equal splendor as ladies of King Louis XIV's time. Laura looked as dainty as a porcelain figurine in silver and pale violet, while Amy wore rose satin, open over an embroidered petticoat, with close-fitting sleeves trimmed from elbow to wrist with frothy Mechlin lace. Unlike her mother, she had eschewed a white wig and had Mariette dress her hair in ringlets instead. No powder, either—it made her scalp itch.

"Laura, Amy!" Mrs. Thurston, resplendent in a medieval-style gown trimmed with bands of ermine, rustled up to greet them. "Delighted that you could attend, my dears. How lovely you both look tonight."

Smiling, they thanked her and returned the compliment before moving on to mingle with the other guests. Glancing around the ballroom, Amy couldn't help but wish that Thomas were with her, if only because seeing some of the more extravagant guises of their Newport neighbors would surely amuse him. She resolved to describe them to him in meticulous detail when she answered his most recent letter.

Gypsies and princesses, pirates and kings, even a cowboy or two. Some wore masks, while others had simply concealed their features with heavy cosmetics. Not surprisingly, most of the women had chosen to wear gorgeous gowns from bygone eras, although one daring soul was dressed as the Statue of Liberty, right down to the *papier-mâché* torch in her hand. Seeing her, Amy was struck with a longing not only for Thomas but for Relia too, or someone else with whom she could laugh over the absurdity of it all.

Still, the Russells had come tonight, as had the Waddingtons, and it was easy enough to fall into conversation with them. Several guests inquired after Thomas, some more slyly than others, as though hoping to hear of a rift between them. Amy only smiled and mentioned that he was off on a painting excursion in New York and would be back perhaps in a week or so.

Once the dancing started, Laura settled into a chair in a quiet corner to chat with the other Newport matrons. Amy, however, accepted a cowboy as a partner in the first set, taking care that his spurs did not catch on the hem of her gown.

Other men presented themselves for subsequent dances: a Roman senator, a dashing pirate, and a Georgian gentleman who insisted on attempting a minuet with her. Despite the masks and face paint, Amy recognized a fair number of her partners, though it was much more amusing and in keeping with the spirit of the evening to pretend that she did not. So she laughed, danced, and flirted—discreetly—with them, though, compared to Thomas, they all struck her as a bit... callow. Still, it was no hardship to take a turn about the floor with them. And to enjoy their attentions when they brought her refreshments—very good, if displayed rather ostentatiously—between dances.

Still, Amy wondered if Geneva had been in the right of it by choosing to stay home with a good book or some quieter form of entertainment. She could write back to Thomas, whose latest letter had arrived only this morning, full of lively descriptions of his excursion to Coney Island. He'd even enclosed a sketch of the Elephantine Colossus. Or she could write to Relia, to whom she also owed a reply. Her twin was still on her honeymoon, extolling the beauties of the West Country and the virtues of her new husband. Either way, grand parties like these were most fun if one had a companion to enjoy them with. Otherwise, they palled a bit—and sooner than she would have imagined, once.

Towards the middle of the evening, she took refuge in a flower-bedecked alcove—fortunately unoccupied—to rest her tired feet. On the floor, the dancers whirled through a lively Viennese waltz, of the sort Amy would have delighted in, had Thomas been present. Beguiled by the music and the motion, she watched the couples, spotting Clara Thurston—a shepherdess straight out of a Watteau painting—in the arms of a Cavalier, and Sally Vandermere, wearing a spangled white gown and a sparkling tiara, partnered with a second Cavalier.

Despite their masks, plumed hats, and long, shoulder-length ringlets, Amy recognized the Cavaliers as Theo Van Horn and Tony Ogden. No amount of lace and feathers could disguise those brawny builds, though she could not yet tell which was which. Strange that they should have chosen such similar costumes, she mused; only the colors of their suits—scarlet and peacock blue, respectively—were different. As both appeared to be pursuing Sally, one would think each would want to set himself apart from his rival.

The music ended and the dancers bowed to each other and began drifting from the floor, the men returning ladies to their chaperons or handing them off to their next partners. But Sally and her Cavalier, Amy noted with a touch of dismay, were heading towards her alcove. Grimacing, she shrank back in her chair, drawing her full skirts out of the line of sight. While she'd resolved to be more cordial to Sally in future, she did not feel inclined towards conversing with her at present. And even less inclined towards playing gooseberry between Sally and one of her beaux.

Fortunately for her, the couple paused before the mass of flowers shielding the alcove, though their conversation reached her ears clearly enough.

"I'm so glad I was able to come," Sally was saying. "Poor Mama developed a terrible migraine this afternoon and had to retire early. But she knows how I've been looking forward to this all week, so she consented to my going with the Ogdens. Wasn't that lucky?"

"Very lucky." The Cavalier's voice was low and husky. "I would have been devastated if *you* hadn't been here."

They were standing so close that Amy could hear Sally's little intake of breath before she resumed, "I do love masquerades, don't you? It's such fun to dress up and be someone else for the night. You make a very dashing Cavalier, Theo."

Theo. Amy's hand tightened about her fan as the Cavalier replied, "And you make a delightful Cinderella, right down to your silver slippers. Though I hope you're not planning to vanish at the stroke of twelve."

Sally gave a soft giggle. "Oh, no—unlike Cinderella, I mean to stay all night! Or at least as long as the Ogdens do," she amended.

"Good. I've been hankering to get you alone all evening."

Another charged pause, then, "Well, you have me alone now, don't you?"

"No, I meant really alone. Just the two of us—just for a little while."

"Oh, I shouldn't, Theo! What if people *see*?"

"They won't notice if we time it right, *and* if we leave the ballroom separately. Come on, Sally," he urged, "meet me in the garden in five minutes—by the fountain, say. It'll be perfectly safe, I promise." His voice took on a caressing note that he probably thought was seductive. "Don't you *want* to be alone with me, Sally—no parents, no chaperon, just Cinderella and her dashing Cavalier?"

Why, that conceited... *Don't do it,* Amy silently willed the girl. *Have a bit of* sense.

"You know I do," Sally responded breathlessly. "All right, Theo. I'll meet you!"

"That's my girl." Satisfaction dripped from every syllable. "Five minutes, then."

Amy sensed, rather than saw them move away, each heading in different directions—for the moment. *It's none of my business,* she tried to tell herself, but her conscience would not stop niggling at her. It was one thing to flirt with a beau or two at a party, even to steal a moment or two of privacy. Young American ladies weren't as strictly chaperoned as their English counterparts. Perhaps Amy had been more influenced than she knew by her time abroad, but...

If Sally wasn't careful, she could end up compromised and obliged to marry—whether she wanted to, or not. Plus, there was a better than average chance that Theo had designs on the

Vandermere money. What harm could it do to follow Sally to the rendezvous at a discreet distance—and intervene if it became necessary? In her mother's absence, *someone* ought to be looking out for her. None of the Ogdens were, Amy noted with a jaundiced eye—not Mrs. Ogden, last seen gossiping with the other matrons, or Mabel Ogden, currently flirting with a cowboy on the other side of the ballroom! Even Tony, whom she would have imagined to be watching Sally and Theo like a hawk, was nowhere to be seen at present. Which was probably why Theo was making his move now.

And so it was that, five minutes later, treading as softly as she could in her dancing slippers, she trailed Sally from the ballroom. Not quite a half-moon tonight, but the girl's white gown and glittering tiara made her easy to spot. Keeping to the shadows, Amy followed her quarry along the path leading to the garden. Ahead of them, she could hear the soft plash of the fountain, glimpsed its waterspout and marble basin, both ghostly white in the darkness. She ducked behind a tree as Sally came to a halt before the fountain, looking about with a half-eager, half-guilty air for Theo. Amy peered out from her hiding place as well, seeking the white plumes and lace collar of a Cavalier.

Then she saw them: emerging from behind the surrounding hedges, the sound of their approach concealed by the soft, dense grass and the gush of the waterspout. Two men, hooded, in dark clothes, one of them holding a sack, the other a coil of rope, stealing towards the unwary girl awaiting her beau in the moonlight…

"Sally, run!" Amy shouted at the top of her lungs, and flung herself headlong at the kidnappers.

CHAPTER SIX

What of the heart without her? Nay, poor heart,
Of thee what word remains ere speech be still?
A wayfarer by barren ways and chill,
Steep ways and weary, without her thou art...
—DANTE GABRIEL ROSSETTI, "Without Her"

NEW YORK, *9 September 1891*

WEARY BUT CONTENT, Thomas climbed the stairs to his chamber in the Newbolds' townhouse and let himself in.

A full productive day and a sketchbook with only a few blank pages to show for it. Perhaps somewhere in it was the basis for the masterpiece he'd promised Amelia.

Amelia. The thought of seeing her again—no later than this weekend—sent a pleasurable hum through him. He'd missed her keenly this last week or so, her hand on his arm, her laughing presence at his side. Her sometimes pointed observations about New York life. Even her endearing—and persistent—attempts at seduction. If she only knew just how hard it was for him to resist, how much restraint it took not to bury himself in her warmth and sweetness...

Or perhaps she did know, and was currently hatching additional stratagems in anticipation of their reunion. And while Thomas had no intention of succumbing to her wiles before their wedding, he found himself looking forward to his fiancée's inventiveness. To her unique mixture of innocence and naughtiness that kept him willingly on her hook.

Setting down his sketchbook and the rest of his gear on the table, he began to ready himself for bed. Some might claim that New York never slept, but in Thomas's experience, even the fastest dynamo ran down eventually. And as it happened, he was the last one awake; Mr. Newbold and Andrew had long since retired for the night, according to the staff.

He undressed, then lay down on his luxurious bed and closed his eyes, yielding to sleep without a struggle...

The moors rolled away from him on all sides, lush, green, and familiar, and a surge of unexpected nostalgia tugged at him like a thread tied about his heart. Devon... the home of his childhood, and looking not one whit changed since then. He half-expected to hear children approaching at a run, laughing and teasing: his brothers and sisters, accompanied by the Martin brood, their constant playmates and companions.

Then, as if the very thought had conjured her into being, he saw her standing on a rise just ahead of him. A slender girl of no more than medium height, wearing a green dress and a paisley shawl, the wind ruffling her luxuriant brown curls.

A face he'd once known as intimately as his own. He'd dreamed of Elizabeth before, but it had been many years since he had last done so, and his memories were softer, more poignant than actively painful. A tinge of sadness for what they'd missed was ever present, but mostly he recalled the affection and camaraderie of their earliest days as friends, before they became sweethearts. In his waking moments, he thought that she and Amelia would have liked each other very much, had they ever met. Both women had brimmed with vitality, had such bright, laughing spirits—and both had been staunch advocates of his art.

He lengthened his stride to join her on the rise and they stood for a moment in companionable silence. Then she turned her head and he saw that her great brown eyes, which he remembered as so merry, were somber now—with a hint of urgency in their depths that stirred his own anxiety to life.

"Elizabeth," he began. "Will you not tell me what's wrong?"

She continued to gaze at him and he saw her green dress—the one in which he'd painted her—pale to white, the skirt billowing out to twice its breadth, while a misty veil settled over her features. Features that were also blurring, changing... the brown eyes turning a deep blue, the shape of the face altering.

And it was his current fiancée's face he saw now, beneath the veil, but her eyes were wide and fixed with terror, her usually radiant complexion nearly as white as her gown.

"Amelia," he said more sharply. "Sweetheart, what's wrong?"

Her lips parted as though she were about to speak. But all he could hear was a thunderous pounding in his ears... no, a pounding in his room, and a hoarse voice calling his name. He jerked awake, lay dazed and stupefied for a moment, but the pounding continued. Throwing aside the blankets, he stumbled out of bed to answer the door.

Adam Newbold stood on the other side of it, his face ashen, looking as though he'd aged ten years in one night.

Dread seized his heart. "Sir, what's—"

Newbold held out a shaking hand—and Thomas saw the crumpled telegram in his fist. "Amy—our Amy... she's been kidnapped."

THE NEXT HOURS passed in a blur of packing and preparation, but by mid-morning, the three of them were on their way. Silence hung over their shared railway compartment like a pall, broken only by the clacking of the tracks and the occasional shrill whistle of the train.

Thomas stared out the window, trying *not* to remember another train journey with tragedy at its end, seeing only *her* face as it had last appeared to him, the bright smile, the steady resolution in her eyes as she saw him off at the ferry. The teasing note in her voice as she'd enjoined him to paint a masterpiece, the way she'd held up her face for his kiss, the feel of her, warm and lithe in his arms…

Other memories, older memories crowded upon the new: Amelia confronting him in his studio, challenging him as no other woman had. Assessing his work with a surprisingly discerning eye. Posing for him in Cornwall, all tart tongue and sweet dishabille in her artfully draped Liberty gown. Discovering his secret longing for her—and literally throwing herself into his arms. Reclining on his studio couch, wearing a sheet and nothing else as she smiled provocatively up at him. *"Must I ask you to kiss me as well?"*

He caught his breath as pain knifed through him, followed by a surge of anger no less powerful for its present impotence. Someone had *stolen* her—from him, from her family, from everyone who loved her, and there was going to be hell to pay. Whatever ransom the Newbolds had to produce would pale in comparison to the price Thomas was prepared to exact from the kidnappers. And from the rage he sensed brewing beneath their fear, he knew that Adam and Andrew felt exactly the same way. If even *one* hair on her head had been harmed…

Never again. No other woman would have to endure this. The abductors should have quit while they were ahead. Once Amelia was safe and back where she belonged, those blackguards would be found, even if Thomas had to tear apart every corner of Newport to do it. And then there would be a reckoning.

He leaned his forehead against the windowpane and closed his eyes, meaning only to rest them for a moment. But when he next opened them, the train was pulling into the station.

THE AFTERNOON WAS WELL ADVANCED, a broiling sun beating down on them when they disembarked at the Newport ferry landing and climbed into the waiting carriage. The remainder of their journey was as silent as the previous stages of it had been.

Bellevue Avenue had never looked more stately and remote, and the façade of Shore House appeared likewise quiet, eerily so. Beholding it, one would never guess that, just last night, one of its inhabitants had been suddenly and violently ripped away from her peaceful existence. The helpless fury Thomas had been suppressing threatened to rise to the surface and he pushed it down again, viciously. Call it breeding or *sangfroid*, but an Englishman—especially an English *aristocrat*— remained calm and collected, even in the face of disaster. Giving way to his anger and fear would not benefit Amelia. For *her* sake, he had to keep a cool head and not act until he had more details of her abduction. Then, perhaps, he would know best how to proceed. Nor must he leave her family out of the equation; they had as much to lose as he. *Our* Amy, Adam had said...

Brooks, the Newbolds' butler opened the front door and ushered them in at once. Easy to see from his pallor that he too was affected by Amelia's abduction, though, to his credit, he carried himself as stoically as any of his English counterparts, informing his master that Mrs. Newbold was waiting for him in the parlor.

Adam thanked him distractedly and strode towards the room in question. "Laura!"

Amelia's mother, her face as white as a sheet, appeared in the doorway almost at once. Even from a distance, Thomas could see that her eyes were red-rimmed and heavily shadowed from lack of sleep. She took a step towards Adam, who went at once to her side. Husband and wife clung to each other in tearless anguish.

"I'm here now, my love." Mr. Newbold's voice was hoarse, barely audible as he buried his face in his wife's disheveled fair hair. "And we'll get her back, I promise."

She choked back a sob, but nodded vigorously, her spine straightening visibly at his words. Remembering Amelia's own strength, Thomas felt his throat tighten. "I'll never forgive myself for not watching her more closely! But she seemed so happy at the masquerade, talking with her friends and dancing...

I never dreamed that something like this could happen, not in Newport!"

"None of us did, my dear," Mr. Newbold assured his wife. "You are not to blame for this in any way. We'll get her back," he repeated, more strongly.

Another woman, whom Thomas belatedly recognized as Mrs. Russell, a Newport matron and a family friend, now emerged into the passage. "Adam. Thank God you've arrived. I've been here since—since it happened. I thought Laura shouldn't be alone."

He raised his head. "Thank you, Elvira." Still supporting his wife, he led the way into the parlor. The rest of them followed without question.

"Tell me everything," Adam ordered, guiding his wife towards the sofa. "Everything you couldn't relay in a telegram."

She swallowed, but nodded. "It happened close to midnight. The last time I saw Amy, she was sitting out a dance in a corner. But when I looked again, she wasn't there. I didn't worry too much about it—she might have gone to the refreshment room or the necessary. But then Sally Vandermere came running into the ballroom..."

"Sally?" Thomas interrupted. "What has she to do with what happened?"

"The kidnappers tried to grab her first," Laura explained. "From the sound of it, Amy wasn't even the intended victim. It was Sally, and Amy saved her!" Her eyes filled, but she managed to continue. "Sally was out in the garden—she said two hooded men with ropes came out from behind the hedges. Amy must have followed her because she yelled at Sally to run, and then... she threw herself between Sally and the kidnappers!"

Dear God. Thomas's heart seized. His brave, wonderful girl...

"Sally ran back to the ballroom, practically in hysterics," Mrs. Newbold went on. "She told everyone what had happened, and we ran out to the garden, but the kidnappers were gone and they'd taken our daughter—" Her voice broke, and she closed her eyes, pressing the back of her hand to her lips.

Mr. Newbold's arm tightened about his wife; his own face was grey and drawn. "Have the police been contacted?"

"Yes, though by the time they arrived, Sally was too over-wrought to give a very coherent account," Mrs. Russell replied. "Half of Newport is buzzing like a kicked beehive over this. The other half has practically barricaded itself behind closed doors."

"What about the kidnappers?" Thomas asked urgently. "Have you heard from them yet?"

Laura opened her eyes. "The ransom note hasn't come, so far. We've been waiting. Waiting all night and all morning too, for some kind of word…"

"It'll come, Mother." Andrew spoke for the first time. "Though I'll wager they've been knocked head over heels by this. They were after Sally, and got our Amy instead." A flicker of grim amusement crossed his face. "I don't imagine she went quietly."

The tension in the room eased the merest fraction. "She upset their plans," Thomas observed. "They'll have to adjust them accordingly." He met Andrew's eyes and mustered a bleak smile. "Let us hope she's giving them hell right now."

"It's *Amy*—can you doubt it?" her brother said lightly.

Mrs. Newbold made a sound that might have been a laugh or a sob. "As long as they don't hurt or mistreat her…"

"They won't, my dear," Adam interrupted, his voice stronger and more authoritative now. "If we're dealing with the same villains responsible for those abductions in New York, which seems likely, then I daresay Amy is safe enough because they want that ransom. We just need to sit tight until they contact us, and then—we can act accordingly. In the meantime," he glanced around at his family, "we must keep our wits about us."

"I'll ask for coffee and sandwiches to be brought," Mrs. Russell said. "You'll need to keep your strength up, all of you."

Laura gently disengaged herself from her husband's arm. "Thank you, Elvira, but that's something *I* should do. Keeping busy will… do me good."

"Very well, my dear," her friend conceded, "but I hope you will allow me to help."

Laura managed a smile. "Of course. And thank you again for staying with me last night. I don't know how I would have coped without you." She turned to her husband. "You, Andrew, and Thomas should go wash and change now—you'll feel much better, afterwards."

"Good advice, my dear." Adam clasped her hand briefly. "As always."

Amelia had always maintained that her parents' marriage was one of temperate affection, rather than romantic passion, but witnessing the exchange between them, Thomas realized the strength of their bond, forged by years of companionship and shared experiences. He only hoped that one day he and Amelia would attain that same degree of wordless understanding—and pushed down the lingering dread that they might be deprived of their chance.

Baths and fresh clothes did, in fact, help, and by the time he and the other men came back downstairs, the food was ready. At Mrs. Newbold's insistence, Mrs. Russell left to return to her own family, though she made Laura promise to send for her if she needed anything.

They sat in the parlor, eating and drinking in stoic silence. Mechanically, Thomas consumed sandwiches and strong black coffee, though the taste of both scarcely registered. He tried not to wonder if Amelia was being fed, though common sense told him that the kidnappers would not starve their "golden goose." Now and then an unexpected sound would have one or all of them starting up, straining their ears to hear more. Mr. Newbold finally insisted that his wife go up and lie down, promising to let her know the moment they received any news.

The knock did not come until evening, and for a moment, Thomas—half-dozing in a chair by the window—wondered if he'd dreamed it. But Mr. Newbold, who'd been sitting on the sofa with his eyes closed, leaning his head on his hand, started up as though galvanized and all but ran from the room. Thomas rose stiffly and followed, Andrew at his heels. They caught up with Adam in the entrance hall.

"I saw no one, unfortunately," he reported curtly, in answer to their unspoken question. "When I opened the door, this was lying on the mat."

He held up a sealed envelope, on which his name had been printed in capital letters. Nothing distinctive about either the hand or the envelope itself, except that the latter bulged slightly at one corner. Breaking the seal, Adam reached into the envelope—and froze with his fingers still inside of it, his face losing its remaining color.

"Father!" Andrew exclaimed sharply, but it was not his son's gaze that Adam sought.

With mounting dread, Thomas watched as his future father-in-law slowly withdrew his hand. Held between his thumb and forefinger, a ring caught the light: a yellow diamond shining like a sun between the horns of a crescent moon...

He could *feel* his blood turning to ice, thought he could hear every molecule freezing, and Mr. Newbold's voice was a distant hum in his ears. "I'm so sorry, son."

Unable to reply, barely able even to acknowledge the older man's words, Thomas took the ring, his own hand closing around it, so tightly that the sun, the moon, and the stars pressed hard into his palm.

THE RANSOM NOTE was enclosed as well, demanding an amount that nearly took Thomas's breath away, but neither of the Newbold men blinked, though Adam's expression grew grimmer. And Andrew, the last to hear of the kidnappings in New York, flushed with fury on reading the stipulation about not contacting the police: the same condition that had effectively tied the hands of the Carrs, the Livingstons, and the Van Allens.

"What about hiring a Pinkerton?" he urged. "Or some other private detective?"

"Not a bad thought," his father acknowledged, "and it may yet come to that, but right now, our first priority must be to get your sister back." He glanced at the note in his hand. "It will take time to get that sum of money together, and it's too late to contact my banker tonight. But I'll telephone him tomorrow morning, explain what's happened."

"Sir." Thomas barely recognized the raspy scrape of his own voice. "I am not a wealthy man myself, but everything I have is at your disposal. And *my* family would be more than willing to help, if asked—my uncle is the Duke of Harford."

Mr. Newbold's eyes warmed fractionally. "That is kind of you, Thomas, but I *can* meet the ransom demand easily enough." He set a hand on Thomas's shoulder. "Thank you for offering, though. Amy clearly knew what she was doing, when she chose you."

Thomas swallowed hard, more moved than he could say by that simple commendation.

"Can't anyone *stop* these men?" Andrew demanded. "After we get Amy back, what's to prevent them from doing this again, and again?"

"They have our hands tied, son," Mr. Newbold pointed out wearily. "They know the girls' families would give whole fortunes to have them back. Money is *nothing* compared to the life of your child."

After a moment, Andrew nodded tightly. "Will you tell Mother now?"

"Only if she's awake. Otherwise... it can wait until morning." Adam's hand clenched about the note. "Bad news can always wait. In the meantime," he added, "you and Thomas should try to get some sleep yourselves. We'll all need our wits about us tomorrow."

The idea of sleep seemed ludicrous under the circumstances, but neither Thomas nor Andrew could deny the merit of Adam's suggestion. In weary silence, they climbed the stairs and retired to their respective rooms.

Thomas lay awake for a long time, however, staring into the darkness—at the ring glittering on his bedside table. Even after he closed his eyes, he could still see it, along with Amelia's expression of wondering delight when he slid it onto her finger. And when he finally slept, the sound of her laughter wove through his uneasy dreams.

~

EVERYONE LOOKED pale and heavy-eyed the next morning, and breakfast was consumed in grim silence. Afterwards, Adam disappeared into his study to place a telephone call to his banker about the ransom. Laura and Andrew both insisted on being present for the conversation, leaving Thomas to deal with any visitors—or further communications from the kidnappers.

A knock at the front door had him springing up from the sofa to answer it. He stopped short at the sight of Geneva Livingston standing on the porch, her little spaniel in her arms.

Her expression registered surprise at the sight of him, but she recovered quickly. "Mr. Sheridan. May I come in?"

Thomas stared at her stupidly for a moment, unable to understand why she had come. Then, like a load of bricks, it dropped on him.

"Of course, Miss Livingston," he said, stepping aside to admit her.

"I heard—about what happened to Amy," she began, a touch breathlessly. "And I can't begin to tell you how sorry I am! I came to see if there was any way I could help."

Her face was pale—this must bring back terrible memories for *her*—but her expression was as fiercely determined as... Thomas's heart contracted ... as Amelia's had so often been. "Thank you—that's very kind of you."

Geneva followed him into the parlor and sat down on the sofa, with her spaniel on her knee; despite his worry over Amelia, Thomas experienced a faint twinge of amusement at the little dog's perfect deportment. "Are Mr. and Mrs. Newbold here?"

"They're in the study right now. The ransom demand came last night."

Her lips compressed. "I imagine the kidnappers want some outrageous amount?"

"It appeared so to me, though Mr. Newbold assures me that he has the resources to meet their demand. And even if he didn't… he'd still move heaven and earth to get her back." *As any loving father would for his child.*

Geneva's blue eyes met his own steadily. "I know exactly what Amy is going through right now, but trust me, Mr. Sheridan, she's safe enough. The kidnappers won't harm a hair on her head because they want that ransom and they stand no chance of getting it otherwise."

Sighing, Thomas raked a hand through his hair. "I know. I just wish there was something *I* could do, personally. This endless… waiting is driving me mad."

"I understand completely. And I have an idea." At his inquiring glance, she continued, "I didn't attend the masquerade myself, but I thought we could call on Sally Vandermere. She was the last to see Amy before the abduction—she might be able to tell us more."

Thomas blew out a breath. "Miss Livingston, not only was she the last to see Amelia—she was the intended victim!"

Her eyes widened. "I hadn't heard *that*! All the more reason we should speak with her!

I tried to see her yesterday, but according to her parents, she'd been sedated and was sleeping heavily. But if she's awake this morning, then she might be willing to see us."

"Do you think she's likely to tell us anything she hasn't already told the police?"

"Maybe. Sometimes, it's easier to remember things after you've had a chance to calm down and collect yourself. Under the circumstances, I should think Sally would want to help Amy in any way possible. And if you or any of the Newbolds accompanied me," she added, "it might be a salutary reminder of what Sally owes to her!"

Thomas felt his lips twitch in the shadow of a smile. "As strategies go, Miss Livingston, that has much to recommend it."

"Well, Amy is my friend, and I too would do anything to help her," Geneva declared staunchly. She gathered her spaniel in her arms and stood up. "I've come in my carriage, Mr. Sheridan. We can ride to the Vandermeres' together."

"Let me leave a message for the Newbolds first, and then I'll gladly accompany you."

~

During the drive to Bayview, the Vandermeres' summer cottage, Geneva tersely related the details of her own kidnapping in New York. From everything that Thomas had gathered about Amelia's abduction, the details were all too similar. The kidnappers appeared to be familiar with their victims' habits and had accosted them when they were apart from others.

"The papers were all over the story last winter," Geneva told him. "Three heiresses kidnapped and held for ransom within weeks of each other. We had reporters practically camped on our doorsteps wanting to know all the grisly details. How we were taken, what was done to us in captivity, every penny that our fathers paid to get us back... they'd even badger the servants for answers. Papa had to threaten to call the police before they'd leave." Her hands twisted in Clementine's lead. "*That's* something to be grateful for—the press hasn't gotten involved yet."

Thomas grimaced. "They might still descend upon us, once word gets out about this latest kidnapping. There are newspapers here as well."

"The *Daily News* is the only one worth bothering about, and so far, it's kept its distance."

"That gives it points over most London rags." He doubted that any American reporters could be as obnoxious or persistent as the ones employed by Fleet Street. "Did the papers offer any useful information at the time, or just noise?"

"The latter, mostly. The police told my father that they'd observed a pattern among the kidnappings, but there wasn't enough evidence to make an arrest or even to name a prime suspect. Maybe Sally can provide a missing piece or two."

"Is it absolutely certain that we're dealing with the same blackguards?"

"It seems the most likely possibility, from what I've heard."

She shivered. "And it's almost too awful to imagine that there might be *two* such gangs out there!"

Thomas rubbed his forehead. "Forgive me, Miss Livingston —I don't wish to cause you further alarm. And in all likelihood, you're right, though these men must be desperate indeed to start up again *here*, where they won't have the same resources they would in the city."

"No, they wouldn't, would they?" she said, much struck by this. "Not the same resources, *and* a much smaller territory! So, wherever they're keeping Amy, it *must* still be on the island!'

"That thought had occurred to me as well. And I'm quite prepared to turn Newport upside-down to find her—though I wouldn't know where to begin."

"Let's hope it won't come to that. But if it does, I would be more than willing to assist you—and so would the rest of the Livingstons!"

The carriage came to a stop at last before another grand Newport mansion. Thomas climbed out first, then helped Geneva and Clemmie descend. Man, woman, and dog made their way up the walk and knocked on the front door.

The Vandermeres' butler admitted them and escorted them into the family parlor, where

Mrs. Vandermere, a well-groomed matron who strongly resembled her daughter, received them with guarded courtesy. She balked, however, when Geneva asked if they might speak to Sally.

"My daughter has been through a dreadful ordeal," she began.

"Mrs. Vandermere, I know exactly what Sally went through that night," Geneva said, meeting the older woman's eyes squarely. "*And* what Amy is going through now. That's why Mr. Sheridan and I have come here today—please help us to help *her*."

Mrs. Vandermere hesitated a moment longer, then nodded. "This whole family owes Amy Newbold a debt. I'll see if Sally's awake and up to receiving you."

"Well done," Thomas told Geneva in a low voice, once Mrs.

Vandermere had left the room. "I doubt *I* could have made that appeal so effectively."

She fiddled with her spaniel's lead, fondled the dog's velvety ears. "Sally and I aren't close, but the Vandermeres and Livingstons have known each other for years, socially. We're both—*older* New York families. That creates something of a bond between us."

A bond that Amelia's family didn't share, Thomas remembered. All the more reason to appreciate the Livingstons' genuine liking for the Newbolds. "I can see how it would," he remarked. "And I'm prepared to follow your lead in this situation."

"Thank you," she acknowledged with a faint smile. "Though I promise you'll have the chance to express *your* concerns about Amy as well."

Some minutes later, Sally entered the parlor. The usually vivacious girl appeared subdued and wan, her face pale and her eyes puffy and red-rimmed. "Geneva. M-Mr. Sheridan. How good of you to call."

Despite her words, her tone was as listless as the hand she extended to them. Geneva, however, embraced her lightly. "Dear Sally!" she exclaimed warmly. "I was so sorry to hear about what happened. Are you all right?"

"A little better now, thank you." Sally sank down onto a chair opposite the sofa Thomas and Geneva had been sharing. "Has—has there been any news yet, about Amy?"

Geneva glanced at Thomas, who picked up his cue. "A ransom note was delivered last night, Miss Vandermere," he informed her.

Sally's eyes widened. "A ransom note? Have you contacted the police, Mr. Sheridan?"

He shook his head as he held her gaze. "The kidnappers have made that a condition of Amelia's safe return. No police."

"The same condition applied for *me*, last winter," Geneva added.

Sally bit her lip. "I'm—so sorry that I didn't visit you then, Geneva. I thought about it... but I just didn't know what to say."

"I understand, dear," Geneva said gently. "And your family did send flowers and good wishes, once I was safe at home again. But you would be helping me—and Mr. Sheridan—enormously *now*, if you could tell us more about what happened that night."

Sally's gaze dropped. "I've already told the police all that I could remember."

"Yes, but sometimes we can remember *more*, when we're calmer," Geneva pointed out. "That's how it was with me, anyway."

"Please, Miss Vandermere," Thomas interposed. "Anything you have to tell us, however minor, might help to bring my fiancée home sooner." He emphasized the phrase "my fiancée" slightly, and Sally looked up again, quick sympathy in her eyes.

"Of course," she said at once. "I'll help in any way I can, Mr. Sheridan! I haven't forgotten what I owe to Amy!" She paused, then continued a little tentatively. "That night... I left the ballroom to—to get some fresh air. I was in the garden, standing by the fountain, when I heard someone shouting my name, telling me to run... and that's when I saw *them*. Two big men in black coming towards me." She shivered, her hands clenching in her lap. "They must have been hiding behind the hedges, lying in wait."

Geneva had paled a bit herself, Thomas noticed. But she managed to retain her composure, though her spaniel whined softly and nuzzled her wrist for comfort. "Did you happen to see their faces?"

"No, they wore something over their heads. One of them was carrying a rope, I think. For a moment, when I saw them, I was... paralyzed. I couldn't move! Then I saw Amy running towards the kidnappers, shouting at me to run, and this time, I did." She swallowed. "I didn't stop until I was back in the ballroom, and that's when I realized that Amy hadn't followed me! That they must have taken her instead! I told everyone what had happened, and they ran out into the garden. But the kidnappers were gone—with Amy!" Tears sprang to her eyes. "She saved me, but I couldn't save *her*, and I'm so sorry, Mr. Sheridan!"

Thomas pushed down a rush of fear and fury. "Thank you for telling us, Miss Vandermere." The words came out hoarse and strained. "And thank you for raising the alarm."

She wiped her eyes. "I just wish I could have done *more*."

"Sally," Geneva spoke up again, "when you were in the garden, did you happen to see anyone else? Besides the kidnappers, I mean."

Sally shook her head, pleating a fold of her dress between her fingers. "No. I told you—I was *alone*."

The slight emphasis on her last word had Thomas regarding her more closely. A case of the lady protesting too much? Meanwhile, Geneva had not taken her gaze from the other girl.

"Was there anyone you were *expecting* to see?" she pressed.

Sally slid her gaze away. "I don't know what you mean, Geneva…"

"I think you do, dear." Geneva's voice was gentle but firm. "I'm not going to judge you, Sally, or try to get you in trouble, but at this point, *any* detail, however small, could help the police find Amy that much sooner."

The younger girl's color deepened at her words. If she wasn't lying, then neither was she being completely honest, Thomas realized. He had no difficulty deciphering Geneva's hint: that Sally had slipped away to meet someone. Might that person have witnessed Amelia's kidnapping? And if so, why hadn't he—or she—come forward?

He leaned forward, determined to add his own plea to Geneva's. "Miss Vandermere, if you saw anything at all, anything that might prove even a little helpful—tell us, please."

He could see her wavering, visibly. Was it concern for a beau, or concern for her reputation that kept her silent, despite her own qualms of conscience and the knowledge of how much she owed to Amelia? Even as he watched, her lips parted…

"Mr. Ogden and Mr. Van Horn," the butler announced from the doorway.

Hell and damnation! Thomas barely managed to suppress an oath as two beefy young men muscled their way into the room. Ogden carried an extravagant bouquet, Van Horn an equally ostentatious box of sweets. Both made a beeline for Sally, ignoring anyone else in the room. Thomas saw Geneva's lips compress in a thin line, though whether from displeasure at such discourtesy or from some other reason, he couldn't begin to guess.

"Tony, Theo." With obvious relief, Sally turned her attention to them. "What brings you here this morning?"

"I just *had* to see how you were, after your dreadful ordeal," Ogden said earnestly, presenting his flowers.

"*I* haven't been able to think of anything else since I heard," Van Horn assured her, handing her the sweets.

Geneva set her spaniel on the floor, looped the lead about her wrist, and stood up. "Thank you for seeing us, Sally. We should be on our way."

Thomas shot her a questioning look, but she gave a small shake of her head. Reluctantly, he got to his feet as well. "Thank you, Miss Vandermere. If anything further should come to mind, please let us know."

"Of course." Intent on her swains, she spared neither him nor Geneva a glance as they started for the door.

But as they approached Sally's suitors, a low, menacing growl suddenly broke from the spaniel's throat. Thomas stared at the dog in surprise—Geneva's pet had always seemed docile and friendly.

"Clemmie, behave!" Geneva exclaimed, but the spaniel's growl only intensified, her lips curling back from sharp white teeth, her small body tense with hostility and obvious dislike.

Ogden glanced at the dog, edging away uneasily. "Geneva, can't you control that little beast?"

Geneva flushed. "I'm sorry—she's usually so gentle…"

Something flickered behind Van Horn's eyes as he too drew back from the snarling dog—something furtive, something shifty…

Thomas was moving before he was consciously aware of it, guided by nothing more than instinct—and a growing certainty. With a speed and ferocity honed by schoolyard fights, he seized

Van Horn by the collar and shoved him back against the nearest wall, ignoring Geneva's gasp and Sally's shocked exclamation.

"Where is she?" he demanded, slamming his forearm against the struggling man's throat to pin him in place. "Where is Amelia, you bastard?"

A second of frozen silence as the accusation sank in, then the room erupted into chaos behind him as Clemmie began to bark and Sally burst into noisy sobs. A corner of Thomas's mind was dimly aware of Geneva trying to soothe both the dog and Sally, while doubtless glaring daggers at her sister's former suitor. *Her abductor.*

"I—I don't know what you're talking about," Van Horn began feebly, though his sudden flush, along with his shifty eyes, betrayed him.

Thomas leaned in more heavily. "The hell you don't!"

"*You* were behind the kidnappings, Van Horn?" Ogden exclaimed, his eyes wide with shock. "Why, you blackguard, you swine—"

"You *traitor!*" Van Horn snarled, as well as he could from behind Thomas's pinioning arm. "If I'm going down for this, Ogden, I'm taking *you* with me!"

CHAPTER SEVEN

O my America! my new-found-land,
My kingdom, safeliest when with one man manned,
My mine of precious stones, my empery,
How blest am I in this discovering thee!
—JOHN DONNE, *Elegy XIX: To His Mistress Going*
  To Bed

EVEN BEFORE OPENING HER EYES, Amy sensed that she was not alone.

She lay still for a moment longer, then risked cracking her eyes open, half-dreading what she would find. But the last thing she'd expected to see was a red-haired girl of perhaps eighteen, wearing a maid's uniform and carrying a tray. A girl who looked absolutely terrified.

Even as Amy watched, mute behind her gag, the girl set down the tray and approached her tentatively.

"Miss, I'm after bringing you your breakfast," she began, with the faint lilt of an Irish accent. "I'll have that gag off in a trice—if you'll be promising not to scream."

Given how dry her mouth and throat felt, Amy doubted she'd be able to scream, though she had no intention of remaining meekly silent either. For now, however, she gave a small nod of acquiescence, and the maid moved behind her and began to untie the gag.

Amy sighed with relief to find her mouth free at last. "Where," she rasped, but immediately began to cough.

The maid helped her into a sitting position, then held a cup of water to her lips and she drank gratefully. The water itself was tepid, but the sheer wetness relieved her parched mouth and throat.

Removing the cup, the maid asked, "Do you want anything else, miss? Some help with the," she blushed but continued gamely, "the chamber pot, maybe?"

"What I want," Amy emphasized each word, "is to *go home*. And to see the men who kidnapped me arrested, as they richly deserve!"

"Don't upset yourself, miss," the maid began, almost beseechingly.

Amy shook her head vehemently. "I was abducted, taken away from my family and friends! From my *fiancé*—how could that not upset me?"

The girl looked miserable. "You'll be back with them soon, I'm sure! Mr. Theo says—"

"Theo?" Amy interrupted, thunderstruck. "Theo *Van Horn? He's* one of the kidnappers?"

A young man of good family, a stodgy but respectable Knickerbocker clan... who would have suspected him? She'd thought him a fortune hunter, never dreaming that he'd turned his hand to something much more nefarious. Was Tony Ogden in on this too? Amy wondered. Helping out his old college chum, or hoping to profit from this wicked scheme as well?

Biting her lip, the maid turned away. "I've already said too much—"

"Wait! Please don't go," Amy entreated. If she could make an ally of this girl, who was clearly unhappy at what she was being made to do... "Please," she repeated. "You *must* see how wrong this is! Theo—and whoever he's working with—they're *kidnap-*

pers! Unless I'm much mistaken, they've done this before. In New York, to three other girls!"

"Three?" the maid echoed, wide-eyed.

Seeing her dismay, Amy pressed on, "Yes, three! I know them all, and they were deeply affected by what happened—one even had a breakdown and had to be put in a sanatorium. I gather Mr. Theo didn't tell you any of that?"

The girl shook her head, looking more wretched than ever. "I worked as a housemaid for the Van Horns, until they turned off about half the staff two months ago! I couldn't find a new place, and I needed the money—for my mam and little brothers! Mr. Theo said he had work for me, just so long as I kept me mouth shut and didn't ask no questions!"

Amy held the girl's eyes with her own. "If you help me to escape, *my* family will reward you. We'll find you a position, and we'll stand up for you in court, if necessary. The Newbolds may not be as old a family as the Van Horns, but we have plenty of influence where it counts—*and* enough money that we don't need to kidnap anyone for it!"

The maid wavered a moment longer, then capitulated, raising her chin with a hint of defiance. "My mam didn't raise me to break the law or help criminals. I'll help you, miss."

Amy smiled at her. *"Thank you*, my dear. What is your name?"

"Eileen, miss. Eileen Molloy." The maid began to undo the rest of Amy's bonds.

"Where are we, Eileen?" Amy asked, chafing her wrists after the maid untied them. She knew she was still on the island. The kidnappers couldn't have taken her too far, not when she'd fought them every step of the way. Not a warehouse, either... someone's private home, perhaps?

"The Sands, miss."

"The Sands?" Amy echoed. "The Schuylers' cottage?" Conveniently empty for the summer, she remembered, and boarded up as well.

"That's right." Eileen knelt to start working on the ropes around Amy's ankles.

"So *they're* in on this kidnapping scheme too?"

The maid shook her head. "Just Mr. Willie, I think."

Willie Schuyler, the older son and heir. Amy didn't know him well: he'd always struck her as an oddly unobtrusive young man, sandy-haired and pale-eyed. Close to Andrew's age, a recent graduate of Yale—like Theo and Tony, though less physically impressive. A young man who, in light of his family's recent financial difficulties, might have found it profitable to turn his hand to less estimable ways of making a living. It made a sickening amount of sense.

And Willie's sister, Edith, had married Frederick Waddington last fall—and then hosted that Christmas party where Geneva had been abducted. Amy doubted that Edith Waddington had any idea of what her brother had been doing. Yet he would have been welcome in his married sister's home— and known his way about the premises. Known how to spirit Geneva off the grounds with no one else seeing or hearing her. Had *he* perhaps been the mastermind behind all this? Certainly he'd been the most prudent of the conspirators, lying low and not showing his face in Newport. And his unprepossessing appearance would have worked in his favor...

The ropes around her feet slackened, then fell away. Eileen straightened up with a grunt of satisfaction. "There, miss! Can you stand up?"

Amy grimaced as circulation returned to her numb feet—all pins and needles. But after flexing her ankles several times, she felt the prickles subside enough to be bearable. Grasping the bedpost, she managed to haul herself upright, take an awkward, slightly painful step.

"I'll manage," she told Eileen, who was watching her anxiously. "Just a bit stiff."

"Lean on me, then, miss." The maid moved to support her. "We'll take the back stairs—escape through the servants' entrance. But we'll have to hurry, before Mr. Schuyler comes to check on you."

They were halfway to the door, when they heard the sound of running footsteps—and froze, staring at each other in dismay. Amy looked around frantically for something with which they could defend themselves. The breakfast tray, a chair, anything...

Then she heard a beloved voice shouting. "Amelia! Sweetheart, where are you?"

Relief flooded through her, making her knees as weak as water. "It's Thomas," she breathed to a wide-eyed Eileen. "My fiancé."

Taking a deep breath, she called back, "In here, my love!"

The door burst open, and there he was. Disheveled, wild-eyed, chest heaving from his run up the stairs: the most beautiful sight she'd ever seen.

Amy took a step towards him, but he was already striding across the room, catching her up in an embrace that took her breath away. Half-laughing, half-crying, she banded her arms around him and buried her face in his shoulder, breathing in the scent of clean linen and *him*.

"Thank God," he said thickly. "I've got you, sweetheart! And I'll never let you go..."

THE POLICE CAUGHT Willie Schuyler trying to flee out the back door of The Sands, and escorted him to the police station to share a cell with his fellow kidnappers. In the days that followed, Amy would learn more about the conspiracy hatched between him and Theo Van Horn. And of how they'd later recruited Tony Ogden, chafing under what he felt to be an insufficient allowance after his parents' refurbishment of their summer cottage. Of how the three had singled out debutantes in their first year, counting on the girls' youth and naïvete—as well as their fathers' wealth—to make them easy marks. Of how they'd chosen to lie low after Maisie's near-demise after her ordeal, only to start up six months later in Newport. And to be thwarted—ultimately and most satisfactorily—by two women, an artist, and a King Charles spaniel!

Now, however, all Amy wanted was to go home, and Thomas was all too willing to oblige her, sweeping her past the police with the high-handed declaration that Miss Newbold would be giving her full statement later. Amy beckoned to Eileen, hovering uncertainly on the periphery, and the young maid followed with obvious relief.

They piled into a carriage and before long, they were alighting in front of Shore House. The front door opened almost at once, and Amy's family stood there, their faces alight with relief and joy at her return.

Her parents. Amy let them embrace her, felt her father's careful hug as though he feared to crush her, felt the wetness of her mother's tears against her cheek. She smiled at Andrew as he took her by the shoulders and looked her up and down, but all the while she never let go of Thomas's hand.

"Mama, Papa—this is Miss Eileen Molloy, who was helping me to escape." She gestured towards the girl, who came forward shyly. "I told her she could stay with us, for now."

"Of course, my love." Adam beckoned to the butler. "Brooks will show you to a room, Miss Molloy."

After venturing a glance at Amy, who smiled reassuringly, Eileen bobbed a curtsy. "Thank you, sir."

Laura, meanwhile, was hovering over her daughter. "Are you all right, my dear? I can have the doctor sent for—"

"I don't need to see the doctor, Mama," Amy broke in, "but I'd give a kingdom for a bath right now!"

"I'll tell Mariette to draw one at once," her mother promised and hurried upstairs.

Some minutes later, after repeatedly assuring her family that she was unharmed, Amy escaped upstairs, with Thomas at her heels. To her surprise, her parents did not make the slightest move to stop either of them. Gratitude towards Thomas for rescuing her, perhaps? Or was it just that they understood that she wanted only *him* right now?

Even Mariette, waiting in Amy's room, was gently persuaded to step aside and leave her mistress to her fiancé's ministrations, though the Frenchwoman departed with a certain glint in her eye and a faintly knowing smile on her lips.

Thomas closed the door behind them, shutting the rest of the world out, while Amy made a beeline for her private bathroom. Every modern convenience, and gleaming with cleanliness: the sink, the vanity, even the water closet! Her spirits rose at the mere sight of it all.

Thomas peered around the door as she was wrestling with her bodice. "May I help?'

Amy accepted his offer with gratitude, shuddering when she finally stepped out of her crumpled masquerade costume. "I never want to see this dress again!"

"You won't," he promised, kicking the soiled rose satin aside. "Now, let me help you with the rest of all this."

His hands unlaced her corset with the utmost gentleness. But then, he must have had years of practice. Amy choked down a lunatic giggle at the thought—the last thing she needed was Thomas thinking she was hysterical.

The rest of her underclothes soon formed a heap on the floor, and a soft cotton robe was waiting for her. Slipping it on, she let Thomas lead her into the next chamber where Mariette had already drawn a bath for her. Steam rose in soft curls from the surface of the water, tinted pale green by the surrounding tiles.

Blessed hot water, gushing lavishly into the tub with a mere turn of the tap! To think of all the times she'd taken that luxury for granted. Never again. All she wanted was to sink into it up to the neck, washing away the grime and the sweat of her abduction... and the fear. She shivered, and felt Thomas's gaze on her, sharp and searching.

"It's all right," she lied. "Just a bit—cold now. I won't feel it once I'm in the bath."

He tested the water carefully, then gave a nod. "You might find it a trifle hot. I can add more cold water—"

Amy shook her head emphatically. "The hotter the better," she declared and let the robe fall to the floor as she stepped into the tub.

The heat made her gasp for a moment, and Thomas instantly gave the cold water tap another quarter-turn. But Amy lowered herself into the tub as quickly as possible, the momentary discomfort replaced by relief. Soap, her favorite scented soaps—just within reach! And a flask of shampoo as well.

She soaped and scrubbed vigorously, again and again, washing away every vestige of the last two days. She was just about to do her back, when Thomas perched on the rim of the tub and took the sponge from her.

"Let me do that." He moved the sponge gently along the curve of her neck, down the line of her back, as gently as if he were bathing a child.

"Mmm." Amy sighed, relaxing beneath his ministrations. "That feels wonderful! I could purr like a cat just now."

"Trust me, darling, no cat *I* know would react with such equanimity to being bathed. I even have the childhood scars to prove it!" he added darkly.

She giggled, then without warning, the giggle became a hiccup, and tears flooded her eyes, spilled down her cheeks.

Thomas cursed under his breath and dropped to his knees beside the tub. "Amelia, sweetheart—"

Amy dashed the tears away with an impatient hand. "I'm not going to cry! I refuse to cry—I'm *safe*, Thomas, safe. And the kidnappers have been stopped, for once and for all!"

"Which doesn't change that you experienced a terrifying ordeal," he pointed out.

She shivered, despite the heat of the bath. "No, and I may have a nightmare or two, but I'll be damned if I let *them* win! They didn't get Sally, and they didn't get a penny out of Papa, and they'll be spending at least part of their spoiled, shiftless lives in prison! The only ones I'm sorry for are their families, because that disgrace is going to be hard to live down."

He exhaled, touched her wet cheek tenderly. "You are the bravest, most wonderful woman I have ever known, and I am honored that you've chosen *me* to be your husband."

She smiled at him, a little tremulously, noticing the lines of strain about his eyes and mouth; the last two days must have been hell on him as well. "I think you're rather wonderful too. Especially when you come bursting through doors looking like an avenging angel! How did you find me so quickly?"

His mouth crooked. "No honor among thieves—or kidnappers, as it turns out! Once Clementine literally sniffed out Van Horn as Geneva's abductor, and I had him by the throat demanding to know what he'd done with you, he was quick enough to implicate Ogden and Schuyler as his confederates. The Vandermeres summoned the police, who arrested Van Horn and Ogden on the spot, and sent two officers with me to The Sands to apprehend Schuyler and recover you."

She linked her wet arms about his neck, drawing his head down for a kiss. "My hero! I owe it all to *you*—you and Geneva."

"Don't forget Clementine."

"Never. I'll have some butcher's bones sent over tomorrow—and perhaps when Clemmie is old enough to be bred, Geneva will let us have one of her puppies!"

"A pleasant prospect, though perhaps there's something else you might like to have first." Taking her left hand, he slid a familiar object onto her ring finger.

She looked at the yellow diamond shining fiercely and felt her courage flare up again in response. "Back where it belongs."

His eyes blazed, almost feral in their intensity. "Just so. And you're back where *you* belong, sweetheart. Right here with me."

They kissed again, the sweetness of it wrapping around them like a blanket.

"Thomas?" she murmured against his lips.

"Yes, sweet?"

She tightened her arms about his neck. "Love me?"

He stilled, absorbing every nuance of what she'd just asked of him. "Amelia…"

"I need you to take it all away!" she broke in. "To make me forget about everything but you—and *us*. Not to let *them* win, not even for a second!"

Thomas swallowed, emotion darkening his eyes to storm-tossed green. "I can deny you nothing tonight. Nor do I wish to. You win, my lady."

"*We* win," she corrected him. "Now, help me out of this tub."

∼

HE WRAPPED a towel around her as she rose from the steaming water. "Some comment on *The Birth of Venus* might be apposite at this moment."

She smiled at him through lowered lashes. "Not very original, but thank you for the comparison."

"I save my originality for my greatest endeavors—such as making love to my future wife." Thomas swept her up out of the bath and into his arms with an alacrity that drew a startled squeak from her.

She held on to him as he bore her from the bathroom to the bedchamber, not even opening her arms when he tried to set her down upon the mattress. "You are not getting away this time, Mr. Sheridan!"

His eyes glinted at her as he lowered himself onto the bed beside her. "How fortunate that I have no desire to escape!"

Smiling, Amy began to unfurl the towel surrounding her. "*This* brings back memories," she murmured, watching the barely banked smolder in his eyes.

"How could I forget? My studio, a sheet, and you gloriously sky-clad underneath..."

"My body isn't new to you as it was then," she reminded him.

His eyes scanned her emerging form. "New enough, for what we intend tonight. And more beautiful, in the way that things we know and love become ever more beautiful to us." He rested his hands on her bare shoulders, and she was astonished to feel the slight tremble in his usually confident touch. "Amelia, darling— are you sure about this?"

"More sure than I've ever been in my life. Make love to me, Thomas. Let us make love together." Her hands strayed to his shirt buttons. "*After* you get rid of all this, first!"

"Most inconvenient," he agreed, and more quickly than Amy could have imagined, he shed his clothes, dropping them in a heap on the floor, where they were speedily joined by her towel.

"Both of us sky-clad now," she observed, regarding him with satisfaction. How she loved his long, lean form! And his usually fair skin had tanned slightly, courtesy of his weeks in Newport. Warm bronze instead of cool marble...

She luxuriated in his warmth as he lay beside her again, skin to skin. Every knot, every kink still left in her seemed to relax and smooth out when he touched her, kissing and caressing her all over until she felt warm and damp inside as well as out. Heavy-limbed and languorous, she returned kiss for kiss, stroke for stroke, quietly exulting when her attentions drew a gasp or murmur from him in response.

Eventually, he paused, balancing his weight on his elbows on either side of her. "This part will be different," he warned, his gaze serious. "I'd never willingly hurt you, sweetheart, but there may be some pain—"

Amy shook her head, at once acknowledging the possibility and dismissing it as unimportant. "It's *right* that it should be different. I *want* it to be different. Complete."

Thomas's hand drifted down, his fingers trailing along the inside of her thigh. "Then... open to me, love."

She obeyed, spreading her legs apart as he positioned himself at her entrance. And first his fingers gently stroked and kneaded her sensitive folds, until she rubbed against them in mingled pleasure and frustration, wanting more. Then, just when she thought she could bear it no longer, he was *there*, fully aroused and erect against her.

Between one breath and the next, he entered her, a gradual slide that smarted at first—he'd been right to warn her about it —but subsided into something almost comforting as her body adjusted to his presence inside of her. To be this close, this intimate, with the man she loved...

"It will be better for you next time," Thomas said, a little breathlessly. "I promise."

Catching her own breath, Amy laughed softly. "And I trust you to keep your promises! But I haven't given up on *this* time yet!" She linked her hands behind his neck. "Show me the rest of it, Thomas—I know there's plenty more!"

His severely beautiful mouth curved. "Insatiable," he murmured, and began to move within her until the slight discomfort built into a cresting wave of sensation.

No—more like a swing, Amy thought dazedly as her breath

shortened into gasping pants: raising you up to the trees and the sky one moment, dropping you down to earth in an exhilarating rush the next. Back and forth, faster and faster... until you believed you could let go at the moment of apogee and soar weightless among the clouds.

She let go, with a shuddering, almost primal cry—and heard an answering cry as he followed her into bliss.

Later, much later, they lay in each other's arms, sated and satisfied. Eventually, Thomas broke the companionable silence, stroking the hair from her brow. "Well, sweetheart—did you happen to see the sun, the moon, and the stars?"

Amy shook her head, smiling as she kissed his naked shoulder. "No, Mr. Sheridan—tonight I saw the entire universe."

EPILOGUE

Conceitedly dress her, and be assign'd,
By you fit place for every flower and jewel;
Make her for love fit fuel,
As gay as Flora and as rich as Ind;
So may she, fair and rich in nothing lame,
To-day put on perfection, and a woman's name.
—JOHN DONNE, *Epithalamion Made at Lincoln's Inn*

MR. AND MRS. ADAM NEWBOLD REQUEST THE HONOR OF YOUR PRES-
ENCE AT THE MARRIAGE OF THEIR DAUGHTER, AMELIA LOUISE, TO
THOMAS MICHAEL EDWARD SHERIDAN, ON WEDNESDAY, NOVEMBER
THE FOURTH, AT ELEVEN O' CLOCK, AT GRACE CHURCH, BROADWAY.

NEW YORK, *4 November 1891*

AMY PIROUETTED BEFORE THE MIRROR, watching her wedding
gown billow around her. White as a snowdrift, voluminous as a
cloud: duchesse satin trimmed with Brussels lace and embroidered with seed pearls. Another masterpiece from Monsieur

Worth, who had designed it nearly four months ago, after she'd first become engaged. Much to her relief, the gown did not overpower her, as she had initially feared it might during her earliest fittings. Rather, it enhanced, like the perfect frame for a portrait. She could hardly wait for Thomas to see her in it.

Relia's reflection appeared in the glass beside her. "You've never looked lovelier, Twin," her sister declared, blinking misty eyes.

"And *you* look radiant," Amy replied, smiling. "James must be elated."

"He is—when he's not hovering like a broody hen!" Relia laughed, resting a hand lightly on the barely discernible curve of her abdomen, well hidden by her delphinium-blue gown.

"Is he hoping for a boy or a girl?"

"He swears he would be delighted with either, as long as it's healthy. But I think he would like it, if our first child was a son." Relia's expression grew dreamily contemplative.

Relia a mother... the thought was as disconcerting as it was delightful. So far, Amy's private interludes with Thomas had not borne similar fruit. But then, her fiancé insisted on taking precautions until they were well and truly married. After that, well, anything might happen then! Even tonight...

She did not doubt that their wedding night would be glorious—Thomas was still apt to sigh over how he'd meant to surprise her, but she assured him repeatedly that she wouldn't have changed what had happened for anything in the world.

Inevitably, perhaps, her thoughts returned to Newport, and those three days that had changed so much for so many. Amy counted herself fortunate to have come through her ordeal largely unscathed, but Thomas had refused to leave her side for the rest of the summer, which—fortunately—she had found to be sweet rather than smothering. And as predicted, he had several sketchbooks filled with drawings from his sojourn in New York. More than once, she'd found him studying some of them with a speculative gleam in his eye, though he hadn't yet decided upon the subject of his next major work.

Meanwhile, Geneva had regained most of her confidence,

and Alice Carr had returned to New York in the early autumn, also much recovered from her ordeal. She made still further progress on learning that the kidnappers had been apprehended, though she was as shocked as the rest of society by the revelation of their identities. Amy and Geneva had called on her soon after her return, and a friendship had sprung up between them, born of their shared ordeal.

Best of all, Maisie had begun to improve—to the point where her family was hoping that she might be able to leave the sanatorium before Christmas. Geneva, Alice, and Amy had all written to her, and received replies back. Likewise, Sally Vandermere had rallied from the shock of discovering her suitors' treachery, and was now keeping company with Mrs. Russell's middle son—a most estimable young man. And Eileen Molloy had settled in well as second housemaid in the Newbolds' Fifth Avenue residence. The most gratifying thing, Amy reflected, was knowing that Willie, Theo, and Tony hadn't destroyed anyone's lives... except their own.

The Schuylers, Van Horns, and Ogdens had opted to forego the shame of a trial, insisting instead that their sons plead guilty to the charges against them *and* make financial restitution to the families they had wronged. In any case, it seemed likely that the culprits would spend some time in prison. Amy could feel no pity for *them*, though she was sorry for their parents.

A burst of feminine laughter roused her from her thoughts and she and Relia glanced towards the other corner of the room, where two of Amy's other attendants were gathered. Like Relia, they wore delphinium-blue, a shade that flattered Alice's red hair and deepened the color of Geneva's eyes. And Clemmie, who had been brushed until her brown-and-white coat shone, wore a matching ribbon around her neck, in addition to the slim leash on which Geneva would be leading her. The rector of Grace Church had been taken aback to hear that a dog would be a member of the wedding party, but Adam and Mr. Livingston had partly reconciled him to this admittedly unusual arrangement. Clemmie's impeccable manners had done the rest.

Mariette approached with Amy's veil, which she placed carefully upon her mistress's head. The misty expanse of tulle and lace seemed to sigh as it settled into place around her.

Laura Newbold, in periwinkle blue, clasped her hands, her eyes shining with sentimental tears. "Oh, my dear, you look like a princess from a fairy-tale!"

"A fairy-tale with a happy ending, I hope!" Amy laughed, turning to embrace her mother.

"The very happiest," Laura assured her, carefully returning the embrace.

Relia handed Amy her bouquet of richly colored autumn roses, then took up her own flowers. "Ready now, Twin?"

"More than ready," Amy declared, turning from the mirror.

Adam was waiting at the foot of the stairs. His eyes widened and he beamed outright as Amy drifted down to him. "There's my girl! *Both* my girls," he amended as Relia joined her sister. "*And* my lady." He and Laura exchanged a very private smile. "It's been years since I've seen so many beautiful women gathered together in one place," he added gallantly as the rest of the bridal party emerged. "New York will be dazzled by the sight."

Amy took her father's arm. "As long as *Thomas* is dazzled most."

"He will be," Adam assured her.

Twenty minutes later, they alighted from the carriage in front of Grace Church, where Amy's parents had married almost twenty-five years ago. Soft autumn sunlight gilded the marble steeple and illuminated the French Gothic façade: a fairy-tale church in which to hold a fairy-tale wedding. Entering on her father's arm, Amy observed that every pew appeared to be filled. An impressive number of Thomas's relations had made the crossing—to see the family scapegrace safely wed, or so he'd claimed.

The music began, a magnificent organ pealing forth compositions by Handel and Bach. One by one, the wedding party made its way down the nave—Amy heard a murmur of amused wonder as Geneva and Clemmie passed, but neither turned a hair. Then Relia, exchanging a last smile with her twin, before starting down the aisle in turn.

Moments later, the organist began to play the "Bridal Chorus" from Wagner's *Lohengrin*. Her cue at last. Proceeding down the nave to the stately melody, Amy saw Thomas standing at the altar with James, both men looking gravely handsome in morning dress. Catching sight of her, he smiled, his eyes glowing like twin emeralds.

Like the sun, the moon, and the stars.

Smiling radiantly into those eyes, Amy quickened her step to be with him all the sooner.

AUTHOR'S NOTE

To paraphrase a quote from the movie "Gigi," some stories are written all at once, while some stories are written *at last*. While I've had the idea for *A Scandal in Newport* in mind for several years, it took a while to push it over the finish line, during which time I wrote two other novellas and a novel—Book One in my new **Lyons Pride** series! With so many different projects vying for my attention, progress on *A Scandal in Newport* was sporadic, to say the least!

Nonetheless, I was determined to see this story through to the end. Although I'd resolved the secondary romance of Amy Newbold and Thomas Sheridan in *Waltz with a Stranger*, I was fond enough of the characters to want to give them a story of their own. And I had become fascinated by Gilded-Age Newport, thanks to books like Consuelo Vanderbilt's *The Glitter and the Gold*, Deborah Davis's *Gilded*, and Gail MacColl and Carol McD. Wallace's *To Marry an English Lord*.

Newport was, in some ways, its own little kingdom for many years. A seaside resort crowded with splendid mansions—two of the most opulent, Marble House and The Breakers, had yet to be completed when *A Scandal in Newport* takes place—and presided over by a formidable clique of Society matrons. Where cash-strapped English aristocrats went in search of wealthy American brides. Where the epic battle of wills between Consuelo Vanderbilt and her mother, Alva, occurred, a battle that ended with Consuelo's defeat and her eventual marriage to the ninth Duke of Marlborough, as Alva decreed.

Naturally, the prospect of such a setting proved irresistible to me. Throw in some elaborate parties, an exhausting social calendar devoted to the pursuit of pleasure, and a whiff of real danger lurking beneath the glittering surface—and I had a story I was eager to tell... despite the challenges that awaited me on the road to completion!

And speaking of completion, *A Scandal in Newport* essentially wraps up **The Heiress Series**, which began with *Waltz with a Stranger*. This does *not* mean that these characters will never be seen again. Far from it: several supporting characters are poised to get their own stories in the future—including Geneva Livingston, who was partly inspired by John Singer-Sargent's delightful portrait of Pauline Astor and her spaniel, Mossie.

My deepest thanks to all of you who have enjoyed my books! I hope you continue to do so for years to come!

A WEDDING IN CORNWALL

AUTHOR'S NOTE

POSITIONING COMPANION STORIES within a series can present a challenge, which was certainly the case with *A Wedding In Cornwall*.

Is it a sequel to Sophie's story, which was told in *A Song At Twilight*?

Is it a prequel to Harry's story, which will be told in *Beauty Takes A Holiday*?

The short answer to both questions is "yes."

The slightly longer answer is that I felt I'd glossed over a few things at the end of *A Song At Twilight*, one of which was Robin and Sophie's wedding. As they are perhaps my most tortured couple (so far!), I decided that writing about their big day would be a nice present for the characters—and for readers who might like to know how it all came about. I also discovered that matters weren't entirely settled for Sophie's eldest brother, Harry. In a family as close as the Tresilians, what affects one member tends to affect the others, so what could be more inevitable than Harry finding himself at a crossroads in his own life just as his sister prepares to tie the knot with the man she's loved for years?

And so this novella was born. I hope readers enjoy this return visit to Cornwall as much as I did!

CHAPTER ONE

All tragedies are finished by a death,
All comedies are ended by a marriage.
—LORD BYRON, *Don Juan*

NOVEMBER 1896, A FORTNIGHT BEFORE THE WEDDING...

THE HEADSTONE HAD BEEN SET in place two days ago.

Head bared, Robin studied it in silence. Even in the dim autumn light, the inscription showed sharp and clear: *Nathalie Pendarvis. Wife of Robin Pendarvis. Beloved Mother of Sara and Cyril.* And under that, the dates of her birth and death.

He'd struggled for a long time to find the right words, the ones that would feel true—and not like some pious lie. Most of the county already knew or suspected that Nathalie had been no true wife to him, that they'd lived essentially separate lives, and that Cyril, though deeply loved by the man who raised him, had not been Robin's son. Nathalie's violent death, however, had left no room for vindictiveness or spite. And while Robin had ceased to love her years ago, he knew she had not deserved her fate.

In the end, he'd let Sophie's counsel guide him. "However

you felt about her, dear heart, she was your wife in the eyes of the law," she'd pointed out. "And the mother of your children."

Children. How like her to remember that he had loved—and mourned—the fragile Cyril as his own. And though he missed the boy keenly, Robin could not help but feel grateful that he'd been spared the shock of his mother's demise. And it comforted Sara to believe that Nathalie and Cyril were together in heaven.

So, in the end, acknowledging the indisputable facts of Nathalie's marriage and motherhood had brought Robin a measure of peace. He hoped it had done likewise for his late wife's restless spirit.

A hand slipped into his, and he breathed in the delicate fragrance of violets. Without looking around, he raised that hand, gloved and slender, to his lips.

"I thought I might find you here, dear heart," Sophie said softly. Then, "They did a good job with the stone."

Robin drew a long breath. "That they did." He turned to face her—his love, his betrothed, his soon-to-be wife—and felt his spirits lift as they always did at the sight of her. The flower of the Tresilian family, with her heart-shaped face, rich dark hair, and those vivid sea-green eyes that were now studying him with the understanding that would only deepen in their shared years. She wore the dark green habit that made her look especially stylish and sophisticated, an effect not in the least marred by the sheaf of purple asters in her arms.

"I stopped by Papa's grave first," she explained, holding them out to him. "And then I thought perhaps... *you* might want some of these too."

Robin's heart turned over in his chest. Sophie's generosity of spirit—even towards the memory of a woman who'd caused her nothing but grief—was one of the many things he loved about her. "Thank you. I didn't think to bring flowers today."

He laid about half the asters on Nathalie's grave, ignoring the small voice in his head that observed sardonically that the living woman would have scorned so simple an offering. The rest he retained for Cyril's grave just a short distance away.

Sophie accompanied him to the boy's resting place, stood

beside him as he set down the remaining asters, rubbed away a trace of moss from the headstone's inscription. No words were spoken, or needed to be. Robin had never been one for graveside soliloquies, and from their first to last moments together, he and Cyril had always known what they were to each other, no matter who had sired the child.

Sophie finally broke the silence. "I am so glad that he had you. That you were close."

"So am I." Among Robin's keenest regrets was the knowledge that Cyril would not be a part of the new life he and Sophie would build. That their children, should they be blessed with any, would never know their brother, nor he them. But then, wasn't it often the case that someone was left behind in such an eventuality? Sophie too, he realized, had her beloved dead—chief among them, her father who'd died when she was still a child, but whose memory she would always cherish. Just as he would cherish Cyril's.

Slightly comforted by the thought, Robin stepped back from the grave and offered Sophie his arm. "What now, love? Are you heading home?"

She shook her head. "Not just yet. I thought I might—*we* might—speak to the vicar and the organist about the music for the service."

"An excellent notion." Music was Sophie's passion and her calling, as anyone who'd heard her sing could attest. It still amazed him that a rising star of the opera stage was willing to settle down to a far quieter existence as a country hotelier's wife in the wilds of Cornwall. But then, Sophie was Cornish to the bone and the seeds of their love had been sown years before the world had discovered her talents.

"Have you a preference?" he asked, as they began to wend their way through the churchyard.

"I thought Handel, perhaps, or Bach."

"What, no Mozart?" he teased.

Sophie dimpled at him. "I don't think I could hear Mozart without immediately wanting to burst into song, and a bride's mind should be on getting married, not performing! Especially as we'll be having a small, intimate ceremony."

Robin gave an exaggerated sigh. "I doubt any of our guests would object to a singing bride, but if you're sure..."

"Entirely. What about you, Robin? Have you a particular preference?"

"Well, I'm partial to Bach. And perhaps the organist will have some suggestions too." Deep down, Robin knew it wouldn't matter to him what music was being played at his wedding—as long as Sophie was his wife at the end of it. Still, it was only courteous to take some interest in the details.

"How are the fittings going?" he asked, remembering that she'd had a dressmaker's appointment that morning.

"Oh, very nicely. Mrs. Cardew has some wonderful patterns and fabrics in her shop. Cecily wishes I'd chosen white, though —partly because it's in fashion, partly because of the old rhyme. 'Married in white, you have chosen all right,'" Sophie quoted, with a comic eye roll.

"Doesn't another part of it go, 'Married in black, you will wish yourself back'?"

"No chance of that, no matter *what* color I wear!" Sophie laughed, tightening her hold on his arm. "I've waited far too long for this!"

"We both have." Years of separation and sacrifice finally, miraculously redeemed—impossible not to rejoice at that. Some might look askance at his remarrying less than six months after Nathalie's death, but Robin found he didn't give a hearty damn. "But, just to be certain, you're *not* marrying in black, are you?"

"Certainly not. Although," Sophie cast down her eyes demurely, "older brides such as myself are often encouraged to marry in *quieter* shades—like grey or lavender."

"Twenty-three is hardly ancient!" Robin exclaimed, taken aback.

"Well, rest assured that I didn't choose those colors either! And although I won't be wearing white, I still hope to dazzle you on our wedding day."

"You would dazzle me wearing a burlap sack."

She gave him a brilliant smile. "And Sara will dazzle you too, Robin. Just wait until you see her in her new frock."

The growing friendship between his daughter and his bride never failed to delight him. And the melancholy he'd felt earlier was breaking up now, like clouds scattering before a warm summer breeze—for which he had the woman beside him to thank.

Drawing Sophie into his arms, Robin kissed her lingeringly, savoring the sensation of her soft lips against his own. "Thank you, my love."

"For what?" she asked, warm and pliant in his embrace.

"For reminding me that life can begin as well as end at the church door."

CHAPTER TWO

Now I've often heard it said by my father and my
  mother,
That going to a wedding was the making of another...
—"Old Maid in the Garret," *Irish folk song*

TEN DAYS BEFORE THE WEDDING...

"YOU *CANNOT* BE SERIOUS!"

Sir Harry Tresilian had heard his mistress utter those words before, often with a note of laughter in her voice, for May was serious about once in a blue moon. But never had she spoken them with such incredulity—that bordered on shock.

"Never more so, my dear," he replied, looking back over his shoulder to where she still sat among the rumpled bedclothes, staring at him with astonished dark eyes. "I should like you to attend my sister's wedding next week."

May shrugged, affecting nonchalance. "As to that, not even the most stiff-necked members of the congregation can bar me from the church—"

"*And* to attend the wedding breakfast afterwards, as my particular guest," he finished.

She ran a hand through her black curls, spilling in wild profusion over her smooth, pale shoulders. Shoulders Harry had been licking and tasting not half an hour ago. Skin like Devon cream, and a mouth as full and red as summer strawberries— and a tongue more tart than sweet, but amusing nonetheless. "And the wedding breakfast is to be held at Roswarne. Your family home, in which all the Tresilians will be assembled?"

"Perhaps not *all* of them," Harry temporized. "Sophie and Robin wanted a smallish wedding. But the immediate family will certainly be there." He added, more gently, "And you will be welcome. You needn't worry that my family will make you feel uncomfortable."

May rolled her eyes. "Not even your sister Cecily? We both know how fond she is of *me*!"

Harry just managed not to sigh. May did have a point— Cecily *was* ill at ease around her, and May's habit of flippancy did not help matters. "Cecy won't make a scene. It's to be Sophie's wedding, after all. And Sophie has nothing against you."

"*That's* because Sophie doesn't know me," May pointed out. "No doubt she'd find plenty to object to, if she did!"

"Nonsense!" Harry did his best to sound bracing. "Sophie's always been one to extend a hand in friendship. And she's perhaps the least judgmental of us all."

"Hm." May did not look or sound convinced. Throwing aside the sheet, she swung her feet to the floor and reached for her discarded dressing gown, a sheer silk confection the color of ripe peaches that no staid, respectable sort of woman would be caught dead in. Harry had loved seeing her in it—and taking her out of it even more. "I highly doubt your sister Sophie and I would have much in common."

"You might be surprised," he retorted. "Sophie is an opera singer. She's had—some experience of the world these last four years or so." Though, if truth be told, Harry did not much like to think what that experience might have included; there were some things he wasn't comfortable thinking about in connection with his youngest sister.

May glanced at him, her expression suddenly sly and a hint of mischief sparkling in her eyes. Reading his mind again, confound her.

He improvised hastily, "What I'm saying is that Sophie has traveled far beyond Cornwall, and they do say that travel broadens the mind—and Sophie was broad-minded to begin with. You needn't fear a snub or a cold shoulder from her. Besides, I doubt she'll have eyes for anyone but Rob in any case," he added with a wry smile. "To look at them you'd think they were married already."

As we might be. As we could be. The words hung unspoken on the air: an old subject, and a sensitive one. One that May consistently avoided… as she did now. Lips compressed, eyes averted, she busied herself with tying the sash of her robe about her trim waist.

"Well?" Harry probed at last, unnerved by the continuing silence.

She glanced up, her lower lip caught between her teeth. "I don't wish to make anyone at the wedding uncomfortable. Or to be *made* uncomfortable myself."

"And I give you my word, as a Tresilian and a gentleman, that neither of those things will happen. Does that count for nothing?"

Her voice was low, but vehement. "You know *just* what it counts for, with me."

"So I should hope." He paused, then resumed, more gently, "I know this is unexpected, May-blossom. But I hope you'll think about it, at least."

She flushed at the endearment—as he'd known she would—and dropped her gaze, but not before he saw the warring emotions in her eyes. "Very well," she conceded, almost sullenly. "I promise to *think* about it."

For all her flippancy, May did not make promises lightly. Taking it as a small victory, Harry stole a farewell kiss before he let himself out of her chamber.

~

HE LEFT by the back entrance, where his horse was already waiting for him. As always, May's grooms were models of discretion—not surprising given how long he'd been coming here—and as always, Harry slipped them a coin to keep it that way.

He looked up and down the lane before venturing out, but, fortunately, no one was in sight. A fair portion of St. Perran might suspect that he and May were keeping company—Harry's own family had long since twigged to it—but there was no need to provide more food for the gossips by flaunting their association. And if it had been solely up to Harry, they would have formalized matters soon after becoming lovers. But how did one make "an honest woman" of someone who showed not the least desire for it? Who brushed off any attempt to talk seriously about the future as if it were no more than a speck of lint?

Nearly three years he'd known her, Harry mused as he and his horse made their leisurely way along the lane. Three years since the widowed Mrs. George Bettesworth had taken up residence in St. Perran, occupying a small property that belonged to her late husband's family. She'd been about halfway through her year of mourning then, keeping decorously to herself for the most part. Harry had glimpsed her now and then, at church on Sundays or shopping in Truro—a demure, black-clad figure with what seemed to be a perpetually downcast gaze.

They hadn't officially met until a ball given by Aurelia, Lady Trevenan, his cousin James's American wife. To celebrate the Fourth of July and her country's liberation from British tyranny, Aurelia had claimed with a teasing glance at her husband. More like *his* country's liberation from ungrateful colonials, James had retorted, though his smile was as uxoriously fond as ever when he looked at his wife.

Whatever the occasion, the evening had been most convivial, boasting good food and drink, pleasant company, and skilled musicians playing their way through a lively succession of polkas, waltzes, and galops. After partnering one young lady in the latter, Harry had found himself in need of a respite. Choosing a quiet corner, he sipped at a cup of punch and idly watched couples take to the floor for a waltz, James and Aurelia foremost among them.

He wasn't sure what had caught his eye—some random movement or a flash of color, but he'd found himself glancing towards whatever it was... and found himself unable to look away.

Over by the French windows stood a dark-haired woman, fanning herself with slow, even languorous strokes. Half-mesmerized, Harry watched the gradual rise and fall of black ostrich plumes, accompanied by the equally gradual rise and fall of a most attractive bosom, just visible above the lady's décolletage.

"Ah, good evening, Tresilian," a familiar voice remarked at his shoulder. "Splendid party, don't you think?"

Adam Prideaux, one of his neighbors, Harry's memory supplied. "Indeed," he responded vaguely, his eyes still on the lady.

"Your cousin's wife has become quite the hostess. Even the highest sticklers appear to be enjoying themselves tonight..." Prideaux's voice trailed off, then resumed in a slightly different tone. "Ah. I see that we share a common interest."

"Interest?" Harry echoed blankly.

"The widow Bettesworth. Comely, isn't she?"

Black but comely. With even features and eyes as dark as her hair, though her complexion was pure cream, lightly blushed with rose—though whether the latter was due to art or nature, Harry could not tell. Nor did it matter, given how delectable the whole package was.

"She's just out of mourning," Prideaux went on. "And reluctant to dance, or so I hear. I hope to change her mind before the evening is over."

Most widows newly emerged from mourning still chose to wear subdued shades like grey, lavender, or mauve. But Mrs. Bettesworth's dark beauty was set off by a gown of deep wine, almost the color of burgundy. Not improper, but unusual—and undeniably becoming.

Just then, as though sensing their scrutiny, she turned her head and met Harry's gaze, dark eyes staring into green. Pure physical attraction shot through him, so powerful that his mouth dried and his palms dampened in their gloves. Not since his days as a callow youth had he experienced this intense awareness of a woman. Even as Mrs. Bettesworth turned away—plying her fan a little more rapidly, some part of him was pleased to note—Harry felt a certainty growing inside of him. He would be asking for an introduction very soon...

They'd become lovers three months later—May's idea, as it turned out, and he'd been at once excited and startled by her boldness. But she'd desired no closer association than that, and after the first surprise, Harry had willingly entered into their present arrangement. As a widow, May had license to do as she pleased, as long as she was discreet. And after years of dodging his mother's attempts to marry him off, Harry had found it a relief to be with a woman who wanted only his companionship and had no designs on becoming the next Lady Tresilian.

He wasn't sure when things had started to change or what had caused the shift. Perhaps it was watching James and Aurelia build their life and family together, their bond deepening day by day. Or witnessing his younger brother John's happiness at finally being able to marry his longtime sweetheart, Grace Tregarth. Or, most poignantly of all, seeing Sophie and Robin reunite, after being kept apart for so long by his past and his obligations to others. Harry could still remember the faith shining in his sister's eyes when she'd first revealed her love for his friend. Barely eighteen then, but somehow that faith had weathered all the intervening years, had still burned bright on the day she returned to Cornwall, to stand with Robin in his darkest hour. And for all his earlier doubts and misgivings about their involvement, Harry couldn't help but warm to them—and envy them, just a trifle, for knowing exactly what and whom they wanted.

It was time—past time—that *he* took a wife and started a

family of his own. And who better than the woman who was already a part of his life, of whom he was already fond?

He'd have to tread carefully, of course. After two years, he knew how skittish May could be when the subject of marriage arose, from which he inferred that her marriage to Mr. Bettesworth had not been altogether happy. May seldom spoke of him, except to say that he'd been something of a martinet and she enjoyed her freedom as a widow far too well to give it up.

But if he could just help her see that marrying again need not be a trap and a trial...

"Harry!"

A woman's voice hailed him, and he glanced up with a start to see a waggonette coming towards him, carrying his sister Cecily, his sister-in-law Grace, and another younger lady he did not recognize.

He touched his hat to them as the carriage drew level with him. "Good afternoon, ladies."

"Good afternoon," Cecily returned, eyeing him quizzically. "I'm surprised to see you abroad at this hour, Harry. Don't you usually ride in the mornings?"

Harry shrugged. "I'd a few errands to attend to. Where are *you* off to?"

"Truro, to help Grace find a frock to wear for the wedding," his sister replied.

"I shall have to take special care to choose the one that's—not too snug," Grace added, a smile playing about her lips. One hand was resting lightly on her midriff, Harry observed. *Well, well, well...* he wondered if she'd told John yet. His brother would be stunned and delighted in equal measure to learn there was a child on the way.

"And my cousin needs a new gown as well," Grace went on, gesturing at the pretty blonde girl beside her. "Gwen, this is my brother-in-law, Sir Harry Tresilian. Sir Harry, my cousin, Miss Tregarth, from Veryan. She and her family are visiting my parents through the Christmas holidays."

"How do you do, Miss Tregarth?" Harry nodded at the girl. "I hope you are enjoying your stay in St. Perran."

She mustered a shy smile. "Oh, I am—thank you, Sir Harry. Though things seem a bit more... turbulent here than on the south coast, especially the weather."

"The sea *is* gentler in the south," he agreed. "On the other hand, our coast is more dramatic. Grace can point out some of our most striking vistas to you, and so can my sister Sophie."

"Perhaps *you* could show Gwen the sights as well, Harry," his sister-in-law suggested.

The hopeful note in her voice was all too easy to interpret, and Harry stifled a sigh. *Et tu, Grace?* Bad enough that his mother and sister were continually trying this, but now his brother's wife had joined their ranks? Three against one was highly unsporting.

"Perhaps." Harry kept his tone bland and inoffensive, even as he privately vowed to make himself as scarce as possible for the next few weeks. By the looks of her, Miss Tregarth was no older than eighteen or nineteen: a pretty child, but to a man of thirty-three, she could *only* be a child. "Well, I must be on my way," he added, ignoring the flash of disappointment he saw on all three faces. "Enjoy your shopping expedition, ladies."

He kneed his horse forward, coaxing him into a trot as soon as they were safely past the waggonette. Not until he was in sight of Roswarne did he slacken his pace and relax his hold on the reins, slumping in the saddle with relief over still another escape.

No more of this, he resolved, blotting his forehead on his sleeve. The sooner he persuaded May to take a chance on them, the sooner he could be done with his family's well-meaning but hopelessly misguided matchmaking attempts!

CHAPTER THREE

What a woman thinks of women is a test of her nature.
—GEORGE MEREDITH, *Diana of the Crossways*

EIGHT DAYS BEFORE THE WEDDING...

"AFTER THREE—WELL, *NEARLY* THREE—WEDDINGS in this family, one would think planning the breakfast would become easier!" Lady Tresilian lamented, peering over the list. "Dearest, are you sure about the pasties? You know Cook is capable of making something more elegant—"

"Yes, but she does make the best pasties in the county," Sophie pointed out. "And they'll be *miniature* ones, so I should think they'll be elegant enough for the occasion. Besides," she added, "Robin's chef at the hotel will be providing a number of French delicacies, *and* the soups—lobster bisque and an herbed beef consommé!"

As she had hoped, her mother relaxed at the news. Lady Tresilian had been skeptical five years ago about Robin's decision to convert his family estate into a summer resort, but she wasn't about to question its success—much of which was due to the hotel's excellent kitchen. "That does sound suitably grand," she admitted. "*And* it takes some of the burden off Cook."

"It frees her up to concentrate on the wedding cake," Sophie replied, smiling. "She's determined to outdo herself on that. I heard something to the effect of four tiers, a pound of sultanas, and a dozen eggs!"

"Good heavens, there should be enough to feed the whole county!" her mother exclaimed. "And I thought Cook was extravagant when your sister got married!"

"I suspect she feels she has something to prove," Sophie confided.

"*Who* has something to prove?" her eldest brother's voice inquired from the doorway.

"Cook—about the wedding cake," she explained. "I think she wants to show that she can surpass any of the hotel staff, not to mention Mrs. Dowling, when it comes to baking!"

Harry grinned, his vivid green eyes crinkling at the corners. "For what it's worth, my money's on Cook!" He turned to Lady Tresilian. "Talking of the wedding, I hoped to have a word with you, Mother. And you, Snip," he added hastily, before Sophie could excuse herself. "Because it concerns you as well."

Mystified, Sophie exchanged a glance with their mother, who then folded her hands and regarded her firstborn quizzically. "Well, my dear?"

He hesitated, looking... almost *tentative*, Sophie thought: most unusual for her confident older brother. "I wish to invite May Bettesworth to the wedding breakfast."

Sophie bit back an exclamation of surprise. She'd never met May Bettesworth; all she knew of her was what Cecily told her. That she was a young widow, who had apparently no desire to remarry, with whom their brother had... kept company for the past two years. Discreetly, for there had been no breath of scandal, but—also according to Cecily—Mrs. Bettesworth was not an easy woman to get to know, attending the more populous social events but otherwise holding somewhat aloof from the rest of St. Perran. Studying her mother covertly, Sophie wondered what *she* thought of Harry's association with this woman.

"Naturally, Mrs. Bettesworth is welcome to attend the wedding," Lady Tresilian began. "But you know the breakfast is to be a comparatively small affair. Just family and close friends."

Harry squared his shoulders, a hint of challenge in his eyes. "*I* consider Mrs. Bettesworth to be a close personal friend."

"I'm well aware of that," Lady Tresilian observed, a touch dryly. "I was *not* aware, however, that Mrs. Bettesworth desired to extend her friendship with you towards the rest of this family. Indeed, I have had quite the opposite impression from my dealings with her."

To Sophie's surprise, her brother flushed. "I assure you, Mother, May has never *intended* to appear unfriendly or discourteous—towards you or anyone else!"

"Perhaps not," Lady Tresilian conceded. "And I can make allowances for those who feel awkward and uncomfortable, living here. St. Perran is a close-knit community, and I know it isn't always easy for newcomers—or relative newcomers—to fit in."

Harry relaxed. "I'd hoped you might understand, Mother."

"Nor have I any faults to find with Mrs. Bettesworth's manners in company," Lady Tresilian continued. "She is unquestionably a lady. However, she is also brittle, flippan... and not always kind."

And the last, Sophie knew, would weigh most with their mother. As Harry himself knew, for he turned just a trifle pale. "Not kind?" he echoed, somewhat apprehensively.

"I was among a group of ladies who called upon Mrs. Bettesworth some weeks ago, to solicit donations to the Foundling Home in Truro," Lady Tresilian went on, her tone as even as a newly paved road. "Mrs. Pearce, our curate's new wife, inquired if she did not love little children. Mrs. Bettesworth replied that she did, especially in a fricassee or a ragout."

Sophie winced inwardly, torn between dismay and a reluctant amusement. She could only imagine the reaction of poor Mrs. Pearce, who—like her husband—tended to the painfully earnest. Not to mention how the other ladies might have responded!

"That was just a joke!" Harry protested, though he looked equally dismayed. "An allusion to Swift's *Modest Proposal*—"

"Yes, I recognized as much," their mother replied coolly. "I was a dean's daughter, after all. Mrs. Bettesworth's remark was certainly clever and perhaps even amusing. But it was not kind, nor was it in the best of taste, and not even a sizable donation could make it so."

"But she did donate," Harry pointed out, though his tone carried a little less conviction than before.

"Indeed," Lady Tresilian acknowledged. "I do not discount that Mrs. Bettesworth showed a charitable impulse. Or that she may have other virtues, though you are in a better position to judge than I. Am I to infer by your request that you desire a closer association with her?"

Harry swallowed. "I—have been considering a more *permanent* arrangement, for quite some time now."

Sophie's eyes widened. Her brother could only mean marriage. Had matters between him and his elusive widow progressed to that point?

Lady Tresilian sighed. "I had wondered if that might be the case. And hoped that I might be mistaken. Not because I dislike Mrs. Bettesworth—for indeed I do not—nor because I think that her flippancy sinks her beyond forgiveness. None of her little... idiosyncrasies would matter a jot—if I truly believed that she could make you happy."

Her voice had gentled on the last words, and Harry's gaze dropped. Sophie eyed him worriedly. It was so seldom that she saw her brother at a loss for words.

"Every mother wants the best for her children," Lady Tresilian continued. "And in our family, that includes marriage for love—a deep, abiding, mutual love. Three of my children have been fortunate enough to find such a love. I should like to see you find it as well, and... forgive me, but I do not think you have that with Mrs. Bettesworth."

He looked up swiftly. "I care for May, and I believe she cares for me as well!"

"But will that be enough?" she countered. "You are a Tresilian, my dear. And no Tresilian *I* have known has ever been content with anything less than love."

Harry fidgeted, as ill at ease as Sophie had ever seen him. "I am nearly thirty-four, Mother. What you describe… if it hasn't happened for me by now, I rather doubt it will happen at all. Perhaps I am destined to be one of the Tresilians who was never struck by the *coup de foudre*. That *doesn't* mean that I could not make a successful marriage and be content in it. Affection may grow, with time." He paused, then resumed doggedly, "There has been no one else these past two years. That must count for something, surely. At any rate, what harm could it do to invite her here, and give all of you a chance to know each other better?"

Judging from their mother's expression, Sophie suspected that she already knew Mrs. Bettesworth quite as well as she wanted to. But her own heart went out to Harry. Knowing what *she* did of love, it saddened her to think that her beloved older brother might be prepared to settle for less. And yet, he was not wrong in thinking he could find happiness, regardless. And as for the lady in question…well, she might not be his family's choice for him, but who would have chosen *Robin* for Sophie herself?

"*I* don't see that it does any harm at all," she declared stoutly, and saw her brother's eyes light up in surprise—and gratitude. "It is just one day, after all," she added, meeting her mother's astonished and not wholly pleased gaze squarely. "My wedding day, and I would like to see *everyone* I love happy."

Lady Tresilian's lips parted as though about to shape some instinctive protest, then, abruptly, she capitulated. "Very well, my dear. As it is your day, I leave any final decisions about whom to invite up to you."

Sophie rose from her chair and crossed over to the desk in the window alcove. Opening the topmost drawer, she took out one of the spare wedding invitations, picked up a pen, and hurriedly wrote "Mrs. George Bettesworth" on the envelope. "Here." She handed the invitation to her brother. "You can personally deliver this to Mrs. Bettesworth the next time you see her."

Harry broke into a smile. "Thank you, Snip! You'll not regret this, I promise you!"

Sophie smiled back. "If it makes you happy, then what have I to regret? Rest assured that your guest *will* be welcome here."

Harry stooped to kiss her cheek, then turned to bestow a similar salute on their mother. "I'll take this over to her straightaway."

He strode from the morning room, a decided spring in his step. Lady Tresilian watched him go, her expression at once rueful and resigned. "Sophie, darling, are you quite sure about this?" she asked her daughter.

"I don't see how I could have refused, Mama. I don't personally know Mrs. Bettesworth, though I admit she doesn't sound like the easiest person to get on with. *But,*" Sophie emphasized, "if Harry is in earnest about her, if he truly wishes for her to become a part of this family one day, then I think we *must* invite her. It would be an unpardonable snub if we did not."

"True," her mother acknowledged, sighing. "I just hope Harry isn't building castles in the air. I can't help feeling that, if Mrs. Bettesworth was of the same inclination, she'd have accepted him long ago."

The post arrived then, with letters for them both. Picking up hers, Sophie felt a thrill of anticipation when she recognized the handwriting: David Cherwell, a brilliant tenor who also happened to be a good friend. They'd performed together at the Royal Albert Hall this past summer, and his letters were often full of fascinating or amusing details—some might even say gossip—about the music world.

Breaking the seal, she drew out the folded pages and began to read with alacrity. Three paragraphs in, she came to a stop, scarce able to believe her eyes. Pulse quickening, she read the relevant sentences over and over, her excitement mounting with every word... until she came to a phrase that was like a dash of cold water in her face.

No. It simply wasn't possible, not with the plans she—and

Robin—had already made. They'd agreed that their marriage, their *family*, would come first. *She'd* been the one to propose it, had not regretted doing so.

She hadn't quite anticipated the disappointment she might feel, however, the first time that resolve was put to the test. The opportunity David had mentioned was not likely to arise again, not anytime soon, not even for a singer of *her* capabilities.

Still, Sophie reminded herself, she was young yet, and there *would* be other engagements. Robin was very much in favor of her continuing to perform. "I don't want you to have to give anything up for me," he'd said…

"Sophie?" Her mother's voice broke into her thoughts. "Are you quite all right? Has there been bad news?" She gestured towards the letter, half-crumpled in Sophie's grasp.

Sophie summoned a reassuring smile. "Not at all, Mama— and I couldn't be better!" Replacing the letter in the envelope, she shoved it hastily into the pocket of her skirt. "I'll read the rest later. We still have to settle the menu for the wedding breakfast, don't we?"

~

No Tresilian has ever been content with anything less than love.

Harry rode along the lane, his mother's words still echoing in his ears and his mood threatening to turn as gloomy as the overcast sky. Family legacies—and legends—could be the very devil, he reflected morosely.

Swans and Tresilians mate for life. He'd heard *that* saying more times than he could count. And perhaps when he'd been younger—much younger—he'd dreamed of that sort of grand passion. Indeed, he'd reached his twenties confidently expecting the thunderbolt to strike at any time. Had watched it happen for his nearest and dearest: Cecily, James, Sophie, and John. And through it all, *his* heart had remained largely untouched, despite the countless eligible women to whom his mother had hopefully introduced him. Pretty women, clever women, whose birth and breeding were above reproach, who would fill the position of Lady Tresilian admirably—and none of them had stirred anything in him beyond a mild liking at best.

Perhaps it was a lack in *him* that accounted for his indifference to their charms. But what good did it do to keep holding out for a dream of love that might never come true? At least with May there was a strong attraction, and—he believed—a genuine affection between them. Perhaps their relationship wasn't the *perfect* union of hearts and souls of which poets sang, but marriages had been based on far less than what they shared. If he could just make her see that... well, he had been patient up until now, and he could be patient a while longer.

Harry touched the invitation resting within his breast pocket, taking heart from the reassuring crackle of the paper. Bless Sophie for understanding—her wedding could mark a new beginning, not only for her and Rob, but for May and himself. His spirits couldn't help but lift at the thought.

May's home came in sight, nestling like a dolls' house beneath the trees. Smiling, Harry prepared to urge his horse to a trot, when he saw the front door open and May step out onto the porch... followed by a man he'd never seen before.

A pang of jealousy shot through him, and he was instantly furious with himself. May had her faults, but she deserved better from him than suspicion and mistrust. If she'd taken another lover or found that she preferred someone else, she'd have told him.

He approached more slowly, his gaze fixed on the pair. As he drew nearer, he could see that the man looked a good fifteen years May's senior, with thinning hair and a thickening middle. If this was Harry's rival, he seemed an unlikely one. But his clothes were of a good cut, and he carried himself with the ease of a gentleman. His accent sounded like that of a gentleman too, though Harry could not yet make out what he was saying.

He rode a little closer, keeping to the shadows and straining his ears to make out their conversation. Then the stranger's baritone rumble ceased, and May's voice replied crisply, "As you saw, Mr. Burdett, there are four bedrooms in all. Naturally, you may make what changes you see fit, to accommodate your family, provided the Bettesworths don't object."

Stunned, Harry came to a halt. Above the humming in his ears and the chill creeping into his heart, he heard Mr. Burdett respond affably.

"It's a snug little house, ma'am, and no mistake! I daresay one bedroom could serve as a nursery for my two youngest, and another for my two eldest. Mind you, I'll need to speak to my wife first, but if she's agreeable, I believe we could take up residence here as early as January."

~

"WHEN WERE you planning on telling me?" Harry kept his voice level, though even to his ears, the words sounded strained and taut.

Once Mr. Burdett had departed, he'd emerged from concealment. May had flushed at the sight of him, though her unwavering gaze had been almost defiant. Dismounting without a word spoken, Harry had followed her into the house to have it out in private.

Now came the reckoning. The cozy little parlor seemed ominously quiet, as though bracing itself for a storm.

May shrugged, not meeting his gaze. "Now that you *do* know, the question is moot, don't you agree?" She turned away to rearrange the vase of chrysanthemums standing on one of the end tables. "As it happens, I have been considering this move for some time. My sister Dorothea was recently widowed. She has asked me to come and stay with her in Kent, for what is likely to be an extended visit."

Kent... as far east as Cornwall was far west. "Why have you not spoken of this, before?"

"I wasn't aware I needed to discuss my every decision with *you!*" she retorted, her dark eyes flashing as she faced him.

With difficulty, Harry held on to his temper. "Not *every* decision, merely those that affect both of us."

Her gaze dropped again. "I—apologize. That was uncalled

for. But I have spent three years in Cornwall already. I never intended to stay so long."

"Why did you, then?"

Her lips quirked in a faint, wry smile. "You, of all people, are asking me that?'

Harry swallowed, obscurely comforted by the admission. "So, if I— asked you to reconsider, and stay longer, would you?"

She looked up, a hint of challenge still lingering in her eyes. "Longer, as in *forever*? As your Lady Tresilian?"

"How did you—"

"I'm not blind, Harry, or deaf, nor am I impervious to hints." Her smile was bittersweet. "The last time we were together, it wasn't hard to deduce that you thought my attending your sister's wedding would alter my views on remarrying."

The last time... the words struck him with an almost unbearable poignancy. What if their most recent encounter *was* to be the very last time?

"And would that be so terrible a thing, May-blossom?" he asked gently, and saw her flinch, just a little. "To marry again—to a man who can offer you affection, comfort, and security?"

She closed her eyes briefly, as though steeling herself for some Herculean effort. "We've spoken of this before, and you know my mind on the subject. It—has not changed, nor do I believe it ever will. For which, I think, we should both be grateful."

"Grateful?" Harry echoed, incredulous.

Her eyes, dark and implacable, gazed straight into his. "You desire me. You are fond of me. But you do not love me, Harry— not as a husband *should* love a wife."

"Do not," he gritted out, "presume to tell me how I feel."

"Very well. I shall tell you how *I* feel." May took a breath. "I care very much for you, but... I do not love you, either."

The words stung, salt on raw flesh, the starkness of them taking his breath away.

"No man will ever matter as much to me as my independence," May continued steadily. "But there are other women who would jump at the chance to be your wife, Harry. I feel certain that, once I am gone, you will find someone far more suitable to be your Lady Tresilian, someone whom your family will embrace. And I wish you every happiness with her."

Harry found his voice again. "So, that's that, then? After two years together—"

"I don't believe in delaying the inevitable," she broke in, almost curtly. "Pray, let us at least part on amicable terms."

Amicable... Harry shook his head dazedly, staring at his mistress as though she were a stranger. He would almost welcome her familiar flippancy over this cool, distant courtesy that made a mockery of what they'd shared. But there was nothing he could say, no protest he could make, that would not make him sound like some lovesick swain trying to hold on to someone who wanted only to be free of him.

Pride came to his rescue, stiffening his spine and sheathing any hurt or distress in pure ice. He was Sir Harry Tresilian of Roswarne, a man of substance, with an ancient and honorable name, who knew his own worth and had no need to whine or beg for anything. Not even love.

"I see you have it all worked out," he remarked with equal terseness. "I commend your efficiency, and I accept your decision as a gentleman should. Far be it from me to prolong an association that is clearly no longer to your liking. However, since you have mentioned my family," he extracted the envelope from his breast pocket and handed it to her, "your invitation to my sister's wedding breakfast."

May's face whitened as she took in the sight of her name on the invitation. Whatever response she'd expected from him, it hadn't been this. "What am I to—"

"Do as you like with it," Harry interrupted with chill formality. "Good day, *madam.*"

He knew he sounded stiff to the point of absurdity, but at the moment he did not care.

She was still staring at the invitation, as if it were a snake that might bite her, when he took his leave.

CHAPTER FOUR

I know a little garden-close,
Set thick with lily and red rose,
Where I would wander if I might
From dewy morn to dewy night,
And have one with me wandering.
—William Morris, "A Garden by the Sea"

Six days before the wedding...

Next to her own home and the beach, the garden at Pentreath—Lord Trevenan's estate—was Sara Pendarvis's favorite place. Especially when the sun was out—as was the case today, despite its being nearly December. Just a few days ago, a shower of freezing sleet had descended on the area, but Cornish weather was nothing if not changeable: this afternoon was almost as bright and warm as a St. Martin's summer.

Perfect for a tea party out of doors, Lady Trevenan had declared, particularly one held to welcome her twin sister, Mrs. Sheridan, who'd arrived in Cornwall with her husband only yesterday. As good friends and even relations of a sort, the Roswarne Tresilians had been invited, and so had Sara and her father.

It was turning out to be a very nice party, with plenty of lively conversation, laughter, and good things to eat and drink. Cyril would have *loved* an outing like this, and Sara felt a pain in her chest at the thought.

Dear Cyril. She missed him so much. More than she missed *Maman*, she had to admit, though she kept that to herself. But then *Maman* had had so little time for her, especially after Cyril was gone.

Sophie, her future stepmother, was different. She really did seem to care what Sara was thinking—and feeling. A few months ago, she'd felt an odd jealous pang when Papa had first told her that he and Sophie would be getting married. But it had lessened over the autumn, along with the fear that Papa woul... well, care a bit less about her once he had a new wife. That was how it happened in all the fairy tales, wasn't it? Except that Papa spent as much time with her as ever, perhaps even a bit more— only Sophie was also there, more often than not. Sophie with her engaging smile and ready laugh, and her sweet singing voice... Sophie who understood how much Sara loved music because *she* loved it too. Gradually, the circle had got bigger, until Sara found herself looking round for Sophie when it *was* just her and Papa.

And there was something else to think about: she wasn't gaining *only* a stepmother but also aunts and uncles and cousins. Even a *grandmother*—something that she'd never had before, because Papa's mother had died many years ago, as had *Maman*'s. Lady Tresilian was lovely and had always been very kind to her. And the Trevenans' children Jared and Alexandra really would be family now, since her father was marrying their cousin. Almost everyone sitting about the tea table right now would be some kind of connection to her, after the wedding. It made Sara feel a bit dizzy just thinking about it—but in a good way.

Or perhaps it was merely that she was still a little hungry. "Please, Papa, may I have another scone?"

"Just one more," her father conceded. "You mustn't spoil your dinner, sweeting."

"I shan't," Sara promised.

Sophie smiled and offered her future stepdaughter the plate. Taking a scone, Sara cut it in half and prepared it the Cornish way, with strawberry jam and then cream on top. She firmly agreed with Sophie that clotted cream was one of the best foods in the world.

All around her, the conversations went on, a pleasant hum that occasionally caught her attention with a familiar phrase or an unusual new subject. A few minutes ago, Mr. Sheridan had made a comment about Parliament—Sara's new governess, Miss Martin, had started teaching her about the two Houses—and mentioned that a Mr. Daventry would be giving up his seat and going abroad with his family soon after. For some reason, Papa and Sophie had looked very serious on hearing that, but neither had said much in response.

Now Mrs. Sheridan was discussing a play she'd recently seen in London. Sara liked plays, though she hadn't seen many, so she listened with interest.

"Of course, most of the men in the audience were hoping to see Mrs. Langley in breeches," Mrs. Sheridan was saying. "I'm sure it was a great disappointment to them to find she was playing Celia and not Rosalind!"

"Well, Celia can be *almost* as good a part, with the right actress playing her," Lady Trevenan pointed out. "How was she, by the way? I've never seen her myself."

"Rather good, actually," Mrs. Sheridan admitted. "Possibly even a little better than the actress playing Rosalind. Though she could have been absolutely dreadful, and they still would have applauded her. Such are the perks of being a professional beauty!"

"*I* saw her last spring in *Much Ado about Nothing*," Sophie chimed in. "And was pleasantly surprised. Given the role and her reputation, I thought she would just preen and posture—but she turned in an actual *performance*. I'd be willing to see her in something again, and not just because she's *the* Mrs. Langley!"

"Mrs. Langley?" Sara's father paused with a sandwich halfway to his mouth. "The clerk at the print shop tried to sell me *her* picture when I purchased yours!"

"And did you buy it?" Sophie inquired, regarding him with slightly narrowed eyes.

He shook his head, smiling. "There's only one beauty for me, my love."

"Too flattering!" Sophie laughed, but her gaze had softened, Sara noticed.

"Well, that settles it," Lady Trevenan declared. "We simply must go up to London sometime, James, to see this lady act!"

"Very well, loveday," Lord Trevenan agreed. "In the spring, perhaps, when the Queen's Diamond Jubilee celebrations are to be held."

The conversation turned at once to the Jubilee, and Sara listened raptly as she ate her scone. At just turned eight, she found the thought of sixty years on the throne almost unimaginable, though Miss Martin had said the Queen had been very young when she was first crowned. Perhaps Papa and Sophie would want to see the celebration, if they were back from their wedding trip by then. And perhaps they would let *her* come too...

ONCE TEA WAS CLEARED AWAY, James proposed a stroll in the garden to help the digestion. Revitalized by food, the children soon took the lead, dashing ahead of the adults along the paths. Bringing up the rear with Robin, Sophie was glad to note that Sara was fitting in comfortably with Cecily's two eldest children as well as with four-year-old Jared. And to judge from his smile, Robin appeared similarly pleased by that.

She glanced towards their remaining companions: Arthur

and Cecily, John and Grace, paired like the devoted couples they were. Aurelia, however, had linked arms with her twin, while Mr. Sheridan was partnering Sophie's mother, and James fell into step beside Harry.

The last could be only a good thing, Sophie reflected. James had long been Harry's confidant, and her brother had been in an uncertain mood since learning of Mrs. Bettesworth's impending departure from Cornwall: morose and despondent by turns, though he did his best to hide it—just as Cecily and Lady Tresilian did *their* best to conceal their relief at the news. For her part, Sophie could summon only sympathy. Harry was such a *good* man: loyal, honest, clean-living, and kind, with a sound head on his shoulders and a strong sense of responsibility towards his family and his dependents. Handsome too, with his athletic build, coppery dark hair, and sea-green eyes. It seemed so unfair that the great love the rest of them had found had somehow eluded him. Perhaps Mrs. Bettesworth might reconsider? Though Sophie suspected that, if the widow had not fallen head over ears in love with Harry during their two years together, it was not likely to happen now.

"Sophie?" Robin touched her arm. "Are you all right? You look a bit—troubled."

She smiled at him reassuringly. "I'm fine, dear heart! Just concerned about Harry," she added, nodding towards her brother and her cousin walking side by side on the path ahead.

"Mm." Robin regarded his friend with sympathy. "A pity that matters haven't turned out better for him. And as someone once crossed in love myself, I wish there was something I could say to help, but I can't think of anything that wouldn't sound trite or banal."

"In Harry's present humor, I think it's better not to say anything than resort to platitudes," she agreed ruefully. "Well, James is usually the best person to be around him when he's out of sorts like this."

They walked on a little further, then Robin spoke again, a touch hesitantly, "Is it—*only* Harry you're worried about?

Forgive me, but you've seemed a bit distracted for the last day or so. And I couldn't help wondering if you were perhaps... having second thoughts."

"About our wedding? Never!" Sophie exclaimed. "Oh, dear heart, there is nothing in this world or any other that could give me second thoughts about marrying you!"

The careful blankness of his expression dissolved, leaving it relieved, though still a touch anxious. "Well, then, what is it?"

It hadn't occurred to her that Robin might be able to read her as easily as she could read him. "Oh, nothing that important. It's just—well, I've had a letter from David Cherwell."

"The tenor you sang with." Some of the tension returned to his face. "A love letter?" His tone was light, but she thought she detected a trace of apprehension in it all the same.

"From David? Certainly not!" she laughed, glad to relieve him on that score. While he'd accepted her past without judgment, she knew it wasn't easy for him to be reminded of the other men she might have chosen during their years apart. "I told you before, he's never felt the least bit romantic towards me. His nickname for me is 'bachgen'—little boy, in Welsh. He's called me that ever since I played my first breeches role!"

His mouth twitched into an involuntary smile. "As an endearment, that leaves a certain something to be desired," he admitted.

"We are good friends, though—and at similar stages in our careers. So, if one of us hears of an opportunity that might benefit the other, it seems only right to pass along the news." Sophie took a breath. "According to David, Sebastian Brand— the baritone—is putting together a production of *Le Nozze di Figaro*, and he's already cast David as Basilio. The company is to play a weeklong engagement in Paris this coming spring, and their lead soprano has just discovered that she's *enceinte*. She'll be seven months along in April, not really fit to travel abroad or up to the demands of the role. David *and* Sebastian think that I should take her place."

"So you'd be playing Susanna? Or the Countess?"

"Susanna," Sophie confirmed. "I've sung the part opposite

Sebastian once before." And they'd enjoyed a brief, light-hearted affair—long over, so there was no need for Robin to know *that*. "But it's out of the question, of course. You and I have planned our wedding trip for this spring, and I couldn't possibly do both!"

"Why not?" Robin sounded genuinely perplexed.

"Because it wouldn't be fair to *you*," she explained. "Our marriage comes first, that's what we both agreed! Besides, we haven't even chosen a destination for our honeymoon yet."

"Paris seems as good a choice as any," he countered. "Speaking as one who lived there for a time, I can attest that it's particularly lovely in the spring. And this sort of opportunity doesn't come along every day. You haven't written to refuse, have you?"

"Not yet, but—"

"Good." His sharp gaze softened. "You should take the part, my love. I *want* you to—and I plan to attend every single performance."

Her heart felt full to overflowing. "And our honeymoon?" she managed to ask, despite the constriction in her throat.

"Oh, that's easily remedied. Depending on which you prefer, we could travel to Paris a fortnight or so before rehearsals are to start or stay on for some weeks after your engagement."

"I have another idea," Sophie said, after a moment. "Let's take Sara."

He stared at her. "On our wedding trip, you mean?"

"Why not? She's part-French—I should think seeing Paris would be a wonderful experience for her. And you would be able to spend time together while I was working," Sophie pointed out. "We'll be away for at least a month. That's a long time for a parent and child to be separated. *I* think she'd be much happier with us."

Robin shook his head, but his eyes were warm. "There's not a woman in a thousand who would propose bringing her step-daughter on her honeymoon!"

"There's not a *man* in a thousand who would encourage his

wife to go on stage during their wedding trip!" she retorted, smiling. "We are unique, sir!"

"So we are." His own smile, the unguarded one that never failed to melt her heart, spread slowly across his face. "I love you, Sophie Tresilian."

"Sophie Pendarvis, in less than a week," she reminded him.

"Believe me, I'm counting the days."

She leaned into him, sliding her arms about his neck. "Let me give you something else to count *now*."

HARRY GLANCED BACK over his shoulder and looked away almost at once. His sister and Rob were locked in an embrace that looked as private as it was passionate. He did not know whether to feel disapproval, amusement… or envy.

James followed his gaze, then looked away as well with an indulgent smile. "I'd say the wedding couldn't come soon enough!"

"I imagine they feel the same." Harry privately suspected that the bride and groom had anticipated the nuptial night by several months, but he neither sought nor desired confirmation of that. At least Sophie hadn't suffered the all too common consequences—as far as he knew—though some might jest that this wouldn't be a *true* Cornish wedding without the bride anticipating a happy event! "For my part, I'll be glad when this whole hullabaloo is over!"

He'd meant the remark humorously but to his chagrin, the words came out tinged with something perilously close to bitterness. Flushing, he glanced towards the sea, a wide ribbon of dusky blue in the distance, conscious all the while of James's heightened scrutiny.

"Has Mrs. Bettesworth responded to the invitation yet?" his cousin inquired at last.

"Not so far." Harry tried to sound nonchalant.

"There's still nearly a week before the wedding," James observed.

Harry shrugged. "For all I know, she may be leaving for Kent tomorrow."

"I'm sorry."

Harry gave a short laugh. "You'd be the only one in the family who is, then."

"It's truly meant," James assured him. "Neither Aurelia nor I know Mrs. Bettesworth well, but she must have something to recommend her, if you've kept company with her for two years."

"Thank you for that. It's nice to hear that *someone* respects my judgment on women. Not that it matters, now that I've been given my *congé*." Harry shoved his hands into his trousers pockets. "The worst of it is, James, what if everyone else was right?"

"Right in what way?"

He blew out a breath. "About how unsuited we are! Damn it all, I thought May cared for me! I wouldn't have thought that she could end things between us so *abruptly*. So coldly…"

"Perhaps that was the only way she *could* bring herself to end it," James pointed out. "Make it a clean break. And perhaps," his tone gentled, "perhaps she hoped to set you free. To find the love —and the mate you deserve."

Harry hunched an irritable shoulder. "The pen to my cob, you mean? Who's to say I couldn't have been perfectly content with *May*, or someone like her? Swans are ill-tempered creatures, at any rate," he added crossly.

"So are Tresilians, when they're ill-matched," James pointed out, smiling. "Just because you haven't yet found your better half, why settle for less? That's not fair to either of you."

"I doubt that my so-called 'better half' even exists. Don't you think I've looked?" Harry challenged, his temper beginning to fray.

For answer, James let his gaze drift ahead of them on the path to where Aurelia and Amy were walking arm in arm, their golden heads close together. "In my experience, love tends to come along most often when one is *not* looking for it." He turned back to Harry, set a hand on his shoulder. "I am sorry that you and Mrs. Bettesworth did not part on better terms. But marriage is for life, Harry—and you deserve better than a makeshift. You deserve the same happiness the rest of us have found. Please think on what I've said."

Harry reached up to grip his hand, grateful in spite of everything for his cousin's understanding. "Very well," he conceded. "I promise to give it some thought."

CHAPTER FIVE

Come haste to the wedding, ye friends and ye neighbors,
The lovers their bliss can no longer delay,
Forget all your sorrows, your cares, and your labors,
And let every heart beat with rapture today!
—"Haste to the Wedding," *Traditional Scottish jig*

The Wedding Day...

"Happy is the bride the sun shines on," Cecily quoted, regarding the overcast sky with disappointment. "I do wish you had a nicer morning for your wedding, Lark."

Sophie shrugged, resigned. "One can't count on sunshine in December, not even in Cornwall. At least it isn't raining!" she added more cheerfully, buoyed by the knowledge that she'd be marrying Robin in just a few hours. *And* her nearest and dearest were gathered in her chamber to help her dress for the occasion. What were cloudy skies compared to that?

Her maid, Letty, brought the gown, carrying it as gently as a newborn infant, and assisted her mistress into it. When the last fastenings had been done up, Sophie turned to face her reflection in the glass—and experienced a wave of astonished delight. Despite all the fittings she'd undergone, she felt as though she were seeing herself as a bride for the very first time.

Mrs. Cardew had outdone herself. Ice blue silk flowed like a waterfall from a close-fitting bodice of pale blue brocade. Embroidered silver lozenges sparkled about the hem of the gown and the demi-train, and silver lace edged the modestly puffed sleeves.

"Oh, *Sophie*," Lady Tresilian breathed, her lovely green eyes misting at the sight.

Cecily was silent a moment longer, just staring at her sister. Then, finally, she spoke, with only the slightest quaver in her voice. "I still wish you'd chosen white... but you do look beautiful, Lark."

"Exquisite," said Grace fervently.

Sophie smiled at them all, her heart too full to speak. But their reaction was even more reassuring than her reflection in the glass. She hoped Robin would be equally pleased when he saw her—more, she hoped he'd be *dumbstruck*.

Married in blue, you will always be true. And she would be. Just as she always had been in her heart, even when things looked their blackest. True to Robin and the love they shared—a love that was to be recognized and consecrated this very day.

Sophie's veil of delicate silver lace had just been pinned into place, when Sara, accompanied by her governess, shyly entered the room. The girl's dark hair had been coaxed into soft ringlets about her shoulders, and she wore a pearl-grey frock sashed with a wide ribbon of deep blue silk, nearly the same shade as her eyes. Robin's eyes, Sophie thought with a rush of affection for her soon-to-be stepdaughter.

"You look lovely, sweeting." The endearment—the one Robin used for his daughter—just slipped out, but Sara only smiled.

"So do you," she said, in a near-whisper.

Lady Tresilian picked up Sophie's bouquet—white camellias tied with blue and silver ribbons—and placed it in her arms before kissing her lightly on the cheek. "There now, my love! Are you ready?"

"Never more so," Sophie declared, returning her mother's embrace. Indeed, had she not been ready for this day since she was seventeen?

Harry, dapper in morning dress, was waiting for them at the foot of the stairs. His eyes widened most gratifyingly as Sophie descended. Folding his arms, he made a great show of looking her over once she'd reached the floor.

"Not half bad," he remarked, a shade too heartily, but the suspicious gleam in his eyes betrayed him. "And I'll wager Rob would agree!"

"No wagering on my wedding day!" she laughed, accepting his proffered arm.

"No need to wager on a sure thing," Harry agreed as he led her towards the front door and the carriage waiting outside. "Let's get you married, Snip!"

~

"Is it hot in here?" Robin asked, running a finger along the inside of his collar.

James, acting as groomsman, shook his head. "Not that *I've* noticed." He paused, surveying Robin with a critical eye. "You look as white as a sheet, old fellow. Take a few deep breaths before you pass out on the spot."

Robin complied, making himself concentrate on the air flowing in and out of his lungs until the light-headedness abated. Impossible not to remember the last time he'd stood in a church to be married. It had been winter then, too: a cloudy, grey morning not unlike today. But there the resemblance ended. He'd been little more than a boy, just past his majority, trying to pretend he knew what he was about. And Nathalie had been even younger, a charming but flighty girl even less ready than he for the challenges and responsibilities of married life. Such a mess they'd made of things between them, in their youth and immaturity—a tangle that, ultimately, only death could undo.

Today, however, he was marrying the *right* woman, at the

right time: his true love and partner, the mother of his future children, who had already opened her heart to Sara. Marrying her in their parish church, before their friends and families, who were even now filling up the beribboned, flower-bedecked pews behind him.

So much more to lose, but also so much more to gain. He understood marriage far better now than he had then, and he rather suspected that Sophie, with her parents' happy example before her, had *always* understood.

His breathing eased, a sense of... *rightness* taking root in his soul. This was what he wanted, what Sophie wanted, and together they could withstand anything life handed them.

"All right now?" his best man inquired.

Robin nodded, squaring his shoulders. "And once my bride gets here, I'll be even better."

"Good man." James clapped him lightly on the back. "I was a mass of nerves too, on *my* wedding day. Then I saw Aurelia, and everything simply fell into place."

Up in the loft, the organist who'd been quietly working away at "Jesu, Joy of Man's Desiring" launched into a stately processional from Handel, and the church doors swung open with an almost triumphant air.

And so it begins. Robin's pulse quickened as one by one, the wedding party entered. To his delight, Sara led off the procession, her small face serious as she scattered flower petals from a tiny wicker basket. Sophie's sister-in-law, Grace, came next, followed by Cecily, both young women looking smart and stylish in matching dark-blue gowns.

An appreciative murmur arose from the congregation as Sophie, a vision in blue and silver, appeared in the doorway, her hand resting lightly on Harry's arm. Robin's heart seemed to bound into his throat as she looked towards the altar, clearly seeking *him*. Their eyes met, and she smiled, radiant even through her veil. It was all he could do not to race up the nave to her, tradition and decorum be hanged.

Not a moment too soon, she was beside him, her gloved hand

in his, as they turned to face the altar and the benignly smiling vicar.

"Dearly beloved..."

∼

THEY SPOKE their vows as though no one else was there in the church.

Listening, Harry found himself compelled to blink and swallow several times. His youngest sister, to whom he'd sometimes been as much of a father as a brother. The sweet-natured, silver-voiced child who'd traveled further than any of them, in more ways than one. Marrying—at long last—a man Harry was, for the most part, proud to call his friend. A man as devoted to Sophie as she was to him. Pray God it would always be so, that the conviction he heard in their voices today would burn brightly for the whole of their shared lives.

It came to him at that moment that *this* was what his family wanted for him too. The conviction, the faith, the utter belief in the person he was marrying and the future they could have. And for all his earlier doubts and scoffings, something stirred to life within him at the idea, something that felt far too much like yearning.

"—man and wife together," the vicar pronounced with a stentorian flourish worthy of a Shakespearean actor.

Not all newly married couples kissed at this point, but Robin and Sophie did, so long and so thoroughly that an amused murmur swept through the congregation. Then they turned, both smiling brilliantly, from the altar to begin their progress up the nave.

Harry followed in their wake, along with the rest of the wedding party. Faces on either side of the church were wreathed in smiles or bathed in happy tears—friends and neighbors who'd known the bride for years, who'd come to like and respect the groom...

Then he saw *her*, sitting in one of the back pews, wearing a pretty ensemble in a soft plum shade that became her dark hair and fair skin surprisingly well. She looked up as he approached and gazed straight into his eyes, as she had two years ago across a crowded ballroom. Something subtly different about her... it took a moment to realize that her smile held no irony for once, and its absence made her look younger—and softer.

A little uncertainly, he smiled back. What her presence here today meant he could not begin to guess, but something inside of him lightened at the knowledge that she'd come. That, perhaps, in spite of what she'd said, they weren't quite finished with each other yet.

Then the church doors opened, letting in a flood of light that left the wedding party blinking and bedazzled. The sun had made an appearance after all, venturing out from behind the clouds to cast a mild but heartening radiance over the church-yard and the newly married couple. Harry saw Sophie tip her face up to the sky and laugh. After a moment, Robin joined in.

Happy is the bride, indeed.

≈

THE WEDDING BREAKFAST was a triumph of good food and good cheer, and Mr. and Mrs. Robin Pendarvis were at the center of it all. They stood with Sara between them: a happy trio, a newly formed family, receiving the congratulations of their guests.

As host, Harry knew it was his duty to circulate and he did so —making sure that everyone was comfortably situated, with enough food and drink to hand, and enjoying the celebration. But even as he exchanged pleasantries, he kept an eye out for a plum-colored gown and its wearer. What if May *had* decided to slip away after the wedding?

Relief washed over him when he caught sight of her, talking with several other women over by the window. Not the best time to approach her—she'd always insisted on discretion in public—but at least she'd chosen to come.

Music rippled through the room, and he turned automati-cally towards the sound. Cecily was seated at the piano, as she had been through so many family musicales. Even as Harry

THE HEIRESS BRIDES

watched, Sophie took up her own position beside the instrument.

"Good morning, everyone," she began, smiling upon the whole company. "I'd like to thank you all for coming today—and for your good wishes. Some of you may recall that my husband and I first met at one of my family's musicales. So, with your indulgence, I would like to dedicate this rather special song to *him*."

Attuned to her sister's cues, Cecily at once began to play a familiar tune. Sophie looked straight at her new husband and began to sing, her pure voice filling the room even as it was clear that she sang just for Robin, gazing back at her as if she were his hope of heaven.

> *"Oh, I dreamt that I dwelt in marble halls,*
> *With vassals and serfs at my side,*
> *And of all who assembled within those walls.*
> *That I was the hope and the pride.*
> *I had riches too great to count, could boast*
> *Of a high ancestral name,*
> *But I also dreamt which pleased me most,*
> *That you lov'd me still the same..."*

At least half the guests were wiping away tears before she had finished, Harry observed; he too was obliged to blink now and then—to clear his vision, nothing more. But as the last notes of the song faded into silence, he sensed May beside him.

∾

"I AM—GLAD that you decided to come, after all."

They were in the library, having found a moment to slip away unobserved. Mindful of the potential for gossip, Harry had locked the door behind them. May's obvious relief when he did so spoke volumes, warned him not to get his hopes up: despite her appearance here today, nothing had really changed.

"It was kind of your sister to invite me, and it seemed

churlish to refuse. Besides," May colored slightly, toyed with the lace jabot at her throat, " I did not wish to leave things as they were, between us. Or to make you think that... I did not care. Two years together *should* count for something," she added, with only a slight trace of her usual flippancy.

"I'm glad we agree on that much," Harry remarked dryly, though his heart warmed a little at her admission. "I hope you have been enjoying yourself?"

"For the most part. The ceremony was lovely, and I can't fault the quality of the refreshments. Moreover, you were, quite unforgivably, correct," May conceded, a faint smile ghosting about her lips. "Everyone here has been polite—genuinely so, rather than in that frozen way people are when they must be courteous to someone they dislike."

He folded his arms. "Consider it great forbearance on my part that I have refrained from saying 'I told you so.'"

Her eyes narrowed into amused slits. "My dear Harry, you just have!"

He grinned at her, and for a moment, they were on the old, comfortable footing again. Then May said, almost too lightly, "Your sister sings like a nightingale. I feel privileged to have had the chance to hear her."

"She's the most of talented of us, musically."

"And she looks radiant, just as a bride should."

"She's waited years for this day," Harry said. "There was a time, in fact, when it seemed she and Rob would never be together."

"So you told me. A veritable pair of star-crossed lovers." May's reminiscent smile took the mockery out of the words. "I'm glad for everyone's sake that matters turned out so well."

"So are we all."

"Your sister is fortunate to have found a husband who clearly adores her," she went on. "And if he's still looking at her the same way one year from now, I'd say their chances of lasting happiness are excellent."

He eyed her narrowly. "If I didn't know better, I'd think you were advocating marriage."

May shrugged. "Oh, I have nothing against marriage, in general. Only marriage where *I'm* concerned." She turned a little away from him as though to examine the nearest bookcase. "A good marriage can be a heaven. A bad marriage is a hell. *I* learned that from experience."

Something in her tone made the back of his neck prickle. "May-blossom—"

"I *did* love George Bettesworth, once," she said abruptly, turning around. Her face was pale but composed. "A very long time ago. I was a sheltered but willful young miss, convinced at seventeen that I alone knew what was best for me. He was almost ten years older—handsome, dashing, adventurous. I thought him quite the man of the world, and was flattered when he singled me out at parties and dances. When he proposed, I was convinced that he alone could make me happy." Her lips twisted. "My parents expressed some doubt, but they were no match for my intransigence. I have only myself to blame for my poor choice."

"You wouldn't have been the first young girl beguiled by a rogue," Harry pointed out.

"Calling my late husband a rogue may be too generous." May straightened, her back straight as a lance, her expression as uncompromising as that of a governess about to deliver a lecture. "I'd mentioned that George was adventurous. As it turned out, some of those adventures involved other women's beds. And when he drank... he could be most unkind. Although, even at his worst, he was always careful never to mark my face."

Dear God. Harry's stomach dropped. He'd known May's marriage had been unhappy, but she'd never related any but the most general details. That her husband had been difficult to live with, that she relished the freedom widowhood had conferred on her. But nothing like this, ever.

May continued, her voice eerily dispassionate, "I'd have left, if I had the means or anywhere else to go. But my parents had died by the time my marriage had become... intolerable. And Dorothea and her husband were living abroad. When George broke his neck trying to take a fence while drunk, I wept. Not for sorrow, for relief."

Harry wondered if it might have been both, but held his tongue, even as his heart ached for her. Two years his mistress and he'd never even suspected. He saw now, how much of herself she had kept back not just from him, but from all of St. Perran. Like a fascinating book, in which he'd been permitted to read only as much as May herself would allow. Perhaps it was a measure of her trust in him that she was finally sharing these dark, unknown chapters with him.

"George was dead, and I was free." May's eyes were black pools in her white face. "And I swore I would never walk back into that prison."

He took an involuntary step towards her, was insensibly relieved that she did not flinch away. "You know, I would never lift a hand to you—"

"I do." A hint of warmth crept into her voice, a tinge of color stole back into her cheeks. "And I want to thank you, Harry, for the—the years of kindness and care. I will always be grateful to you for that—for how our time together... helped me to become less *afraid*. Of men, of intimacy, of my own judgment." She took a breath, visibly steeling herself. "But you must see that I can never make myself that vulnerable again. Never put myself in a man's power again. Even as good a man as you."

His eyes stung. "I wish I could make you see that marriage needn't be the trap you fear."

"I suspect that's a task beyond any man's capability." May's smile was tinged with sadness. "I *must* be free to walk away. I cannot... let myself become close to anyone without knowing that I can leave whenever I choose, with no pledges or promises, no obligations or encumbrances. I know how selfish that sounds, but there it is. Could *you* live on such terms? The truth, Harry," she added, sounding unwontedly stern. "I wish you to be entirely honest with me. Does this resemble, in any way, *your* idea of marriage?"

Harry was silent, thinking of all the marriages he'd seen over the years, the ones that had shaped his own perception of what sharing a life meant. "No," he conceded at last, on a long breath, and the whole room seemed to sigh with him. "Not even close."

"That's what I thought." Her eyes were very bright, but not with mockery. "But what I shrink from—marriage, children, commitment... that is what I want for *you*. Because you deserve it, even though I cannot be the one to give it to you. And because —" she broke off, as flushed now as she had been pale before.

"Because?" Harry prompted gently.

Her color deepened but her gaze never wavered. "Because... I do love you, Harry. Even if it's not the sort of love to build a life upon."

The last ice about his heart thawed. "And I love you, May-blossom. Even if it's not enough to convince you to stay." He paused to swallow, strove for a light tone. "When—do you mean to leave Cornwall?"

"Within the next fortnight," she replied. "Dorothea's invited me to spend Christmas with her. I believe I can have my own belongings packed up and ready by then."

Let her go. Harry swallowed again. "I shall miss you, May. And I wish you every happiness in your new life."

Her dark eyes glistened, suspiciously liquid. "And I wish you the very same, my dear."

He cleared his throat. "May I—may I kiss you goodbye?"

The old bewitching smile curved her lips. "I was hoping that you would."

They met halfway, and he drew her into his arms, his lips unfolding against hers in a kiss that sought to convey all he felt in that moment: affection, regret... and, finally, acceptance. May's response was equally tender—and no less final.

They parted at last, damp-eyed but smiling fondly. May reached up to brush back a lock of his hair. "I should go, I suppose."

"Stay until the cake is served," he urged. "I should hate for you to miss Cook's triumph."

And "triumph" was not too strong a word. The wedding cake was four tiers high: a rich, dark fruitcake frosted in white, with candied violets scattered across the top. Harry had observed several guests regarding it admiringly—and several children eyeing it acquisitively.

"It certainly looked impressive. Very well, my dear." May's eyes glinted with fond amusement. "Far be it from me to turn up my nose at a slice of wedding cake!"

EPILOGUE

Gallop apace you fiery-footed steeds,
Towards Phoebus' lodging! Such a wagoner
As Phaëton would whip you to the west
And bring in cloudy night immediately.
—WILLIAM SHAKESPEARE, *Romeo and Juliet*

THE WEDDING NIGHT...

THE CAKE HAD BEEN SERVED, the speeches made, and the toasts drunk. Now all that remained, Robin mused, was for the bride and groom to make a stealthy departure.

He glanced up the stairs. Not ten minutes ago, Sophie, accompanied by her mother and sister, had slipped away to change into her "going-away" dress—and, he suspected, to have some private time with her family. Eager though he was to be alone with her, Robin understood. He'd always admired and sometimes envied the closeness between the Tresilians. He felt touched and honored at being included, along with Sara, in their family circle now.

A hand descended on his shoulder and he turned his head to

see Harry—his brother-in-law!—smiling at him. "You seem uncommon anxious, Rob. Is all well?"

"Very well," Robin assured, returning his smile. "I'm just waiting for my wife." He marveled at the easy way the words slipped off his tongue.

Harry grinned. "Impatiently, by the look of you. But then, you and Sophie have had to wait longer than most."

Their eyes met in a glance of perfect understanding.

"Harry," Robin began, "I want to thank you for your support today. I know you weren't best pleased when Sophie and I first... took up with each other. And even less so when you learned about Nathalie." That revelation had, in fact, strained their friendship for a couple of years. "But I hope you realize how very much I love your sister. And how determined I am to see that she never regrets our marriage."

Harry cleared his throat, looking slightly embarrassed, but pleased too, Robin thought. "The past is—it's all water under the bridge, Rob. As for the rest . . . well, a blind man could see how you and Sophie feel about each other. Just make her happy."

"I plan to make that my life's work," Robin promised.

They clasped hands, two friends who were now family. After a moment, Robin ventured, "And your own suit—does it prosper?" He'd glimpsed Mrs. Bettesworth from a distance, had seen Harry in conversation with her at one point, but could discern nothing from their exchange.

Harry's lips tightened. "Not exactly. She leaves Cornwall in a fortnight."

"I'm sorry."

"As am I, but it can't be helped. She and I want—very different things from life, and we'll not find them with each other. At least we parted as friends." Harry sighed, looking resigned, if not precisely happy. "Let's not dwell on it. This is your day—yours and Sophie's. I've no wish to be the death's head at the feast."

"Of course," Robin said at once, relieved to let the subject drop.

A young couple with a child in tow approached Harry to take

their leave, and as a good host, he went to escort them out. Reminded of his own daughter, Robin abandoned the stairs to go in search of her. He found her in the parlor, trying to coax Tatiana, Sophie's pampered Russian Grey cat, out from under a chair.

"Sophie was keeping her in the dressing room," Sara reported. "But she must have got out while we were all at church, and now she won't let herself be taken back upstairs!" She placed half of a fish paste sandwich in front of the chair. A dainty paw darted out and snagged the morsel, but the rest of the cat remained hidden from view.

Robin smothered a smile. "She'll come out when she's good and ready, sweeting—probably after the guests have gone. Cats can be contrary that way." He sat down on the floor, put his arm around his daughter. "Have you enjoyed yourself today?"

Her face lit up. "Oh, yes, Papa! It's been lovely. The flowers, the music, *and* my new frock…" She smoothed the pearl-grey skirt almost reverently. Up until last month, she'd worn black— as she had since Cyril's death last January—but Robin had seen no harm in relaxing the strictures of mourning for an eight-year-old girl, especially at a wedding.

"You looked beautiful," he told her. "And you did a splendid job strewing the flowers."

She smiled up at him. "You and Sophie won't be away too long, will you?"

"Just a few days," he assured her. "And in the meantime, you'll have your new grandmother and all your uncles and aunts and cousins to keep you company here at Roswarne!"

"Oh, I know *that*! It's just that I'm looking forward to the three of us being a real family."

A real family. Robin's own spirits soared at the prospect, and he hugged Sara closer. "So am I, my darling. So am I."

Then he heard what he had been listening for: feminine laughter and feminine voices, Sophie's soaring as effortlessly as a songbird's over the rest. He stood up, offering Sara his hand, and together they hurried towards the entrance hall.

Sophie, wearing a smart traveling suit of jade-green wool,

was descending the stairs. Family and friends clustered at the foot of the staircase, eager to offer the bride a parting kiss or embrace. Sophie returned their salutes heartily, stooped to kiss Sara's cheek, and then turned to Robin, who held out his arm.

"Ready to come with me, my love?" he asked, pitching his voice for her ears alone.

Her smile outshone the sun, the moon, and the stars. "To the ends of the earth, dear heart."

∾

"So, where are we going for our wedding night?" Sophie asked, nestling in the circle of her husband's arm as their coach rolled smoothly along the country lanes.

"Some place considerably closer than the ends of the earth," he assured her.

"Care to be more specific than that?"

Robin grinned like a schoolboy. "Not just at present. I've a mind to surprise you a little."

Intrigued, Sophie regarded him more closely. This playful mood was unusual for him, but it should be encouraged, she decided. "Very well. Far be it from me to spoil a surprise." She settled back against his shoulder. "This reminds me a bit of our excursion to the Cotswolds, remember?"

His arm tightened about her. "I remember everything, Mrs. Pendarvis."

"Mrs. Pendarvis." Sophie sighed. "I do love the way that sounds."

"So do I. But even more I love the way 'Mrs. Pendarvis' *feels*." He stroked her cheek, trailed a finger down the line of her throat. "Which, to my way of thinking, is warm, soft, and wonderfully inviting."

"Why, Mr. Pendarvis, you'll have me blushing like a schoolgirl!"

"I hope so. And I hope that a husband may be privileged to see just how far that blush goes . . ." His hand slipped down to

156

cup her breast, one thumb skimming over her nipple, which peaked immediately at his touch.

Sophie bit back a gasp, pressed eagerly against him. Between wedding preparations and Robin's responsibilities at the hotel, it had been weeks since they'd shared a bed. "It occurs to me," she began, a little breathlessly, "that making love in a carriage is among the things we have yet to do. Could we—"

"Sadly, no." His attentions to her ceased abruptly, and he gave her an apologetic grimace. "We've made better time than I expected, my love."

At his nod, she leaned forward and peered out the carriage window. "That's Chenoweth!" she exclaimed, recognizing the redbrick manor house at the top of the gently curving drive. James's house, the one he'd lived in before his accession to the earldom, built by his father for his Tresilian bride, Sophie's Aunt Carenza.

"It is," Robin confirmed. "He's lent it to us for the night, and the following week, should we care to stay that long. Does it please you?" he added, a trifle anxiously. "We could stay elsewhere if you'd prefer."

Sophie shook her head, smiling. "No, it's lovely! James and Aurelia spent their own wedding night here, and they've been so happy together. I'd like to think it will be a good omen for us as well."

"I'm glad you approve. And talking of James and Aurelia, they've assured me that this house possesses every imaginable comfort. Especially," his voice grew low and intimate, "in the bedchamber."

Sophie gazed at him from under her lashes. "Then what more could we possibly require?"

The carriage came to a stop before the front steps. Robin climbed out first, then handed Sophie down—just before catching her up into his arms.

"Robin!" It emerged almost as a squeak, and she clutched at him reflexively. "What are you doing?"

Again he grinned boyishly. "Complying with tradition. This may not be *our* house, but it has a threshold nonetheless."

"There's no need for all this!" she protested, half-laughing.

"On the contrary," he replied as he carried her towards the steps, "this is my second and last marriage, and I intend to do everything right this time."

She smiled, winding her arms about his neck. "Dear heart, I'd say you already have."

∾

SEVERAL YEARS EARLIER, James had engaged Mr. and Mrs. Penrose, a middle-aged couple, to look after Chenoweth. They welcomed the newlyweds warmly and offered refreshment, which Robin declined. After such a busy day, he and his bride found themselves in need of rest, though a light supper—much later—would be appreciated. He and Sophie were subsequently escorted upstairs to adjoining chambers and left to their own devices.

In her pretty blue-and-cream chamber, Sophie sponged herself down with warm water—to which she'd added a drop of essence of violet—before donning the rose silk negligee that Robin especially admired. Despite its sheerness she felt no chill, thanks to the fire burning brightly on the hearth. She was just brushing out her hair before the vanity, when she heard a light knock on the connecting door.

Smiling, she laid down the brush. "Come in."

The door opened, and Robin padded in, soundless as a shadow in his robe and slippers.

Sophie sat where she was, feasting her eyes on the sight of him. Her husband. The man she'd loved since she was seventeen. Sometimes in vain, she'd feared—yet here they were, six years later, their future before them and all the heartache, separation, and self-denial behind them. Here, on their wedding night. If that wasn't a happy ending, she didn't know what was.

His midnight-blue eyes widened in appreciation when he saw what she was wearing. "And I thought you looked beautiful on our wedding *day*."

"It's not yet night," Sophie pointed out, rising from her chair in a whisper of gossamer. "Do you think the Penroses will be shocked—that we've gone to bed so early?"

"Given how long they've been married, I doubt they'd be shocked by anything of the sort." He drew her to him, his hands skimming down her bare arms. "And I think, if you'll agree, that it is not *too* early."

Sophie swallowed, desire coursing through her at his touch, and reached out to untie the sash of his robe. By now she knew his body intimately, as he knew hers, but the sight of his naked form still made her mouth dry and her pulse quicken. Long, lean, hard-muscled—and most gratifyingly erect, though that part of him currently wore a rubber sheath. Sophie had taken similar precautions; they had both agreed to wait until their family was more settled and secure before trying for another child.

In any case, preventive measures did nothing to lessen their ardor, perhaps even heightened it. Robin's eyes kindled as he removed her negligee, sent it sliding to the floor alongside his robe. Sophie caught her breath at the promise she saw there, even as a small part of her wondered how things would be now that the knot was officially tied.

Then she had no time left to wonder, because he was kissing her, over and over again, the heated caress of his mouth stealing her breath and clouding her senses. She leaned into him, returning his kisses just as passionately, running her hands over every part of him she could reach and reveling at the familiar textures of his hair and skin.

The first time they made love, they'd never reached the bed. This time, they sank together onto the cool, lavender-scented linens, lying skin to skin as they continued to kiss and fondle. Some definite advantages to familiarity, Sophie thought hazily as Robin's fingers stroked her in a place that never failed to coax a response from her—a throaty purr like Tatiana's when she was having her tummy rubbed.

Her body was still humming from his attentions, anticipating the deeper fulfillment to come, when he drew back just a little, to smile down into her eyes.

"Tonight," he said, "I intend to kiss *every* inch of you, my wife."

She pulled him down to her until his lips rested on hers. "Then start *here*, husband."

~

LATER, when the grey of twilight had stolen into the room, Sophie roused and stretched luxuriously—replete, she thought with drowsy contentment, as only a woman who'd been thoroughly made love to could be. The gold band on her finger shone even in the gloom, and she smiled at the sight of it.

Robin had made good on his promise, and she'd been more than willing to return the favor. They'd pleasured each other with lips, tongues, and hands, fanning the flames between them ever higher until the moment he had entered her, sliding home in a single powerful thrust, and the conflagration had consumed them both. Afterward, they'd drifted off to sleep, still entwined, lulled by the rhythm of each other's breathing.

Attuned, it seemed, to her every movement, her husband stirred beside her. "Happy, my darling?" he inquired, his hand trailing over her back in a slow, sensuous caress.

"Oh, yes—completely." Sophie snuggled closer, pillowing her head upon his chest. "Although…"

"Although?" he prompted, regarding her with just a trace of anxiety.

"Well," she began judiciously, "I couldn't help wondering—before—if our wedding night would be the equal of what we'd shared in the Cotswolds."

Robin's brows drew together, just a little. "And was it?"

"No." She gave him a dimpled smile, then embraced him with all her might. "It was even better!"

THE TENANT OF TIDEWATER COTTAGE

I like this place
And willingly could waste my time in it.
—WILLIAM SHAKESPEARE, *As You Like It*

CORNWALL, *April 1897*

NOTHING LIKE AN EARLY MORNING RIDE to whet the appetite, Harry decided as he strode into the breakfast parlor. He hoped that Cook had made kedgeree today, along with her usual offerings of ham, eggs, and potatoes.

His mother, the only other occupant of the room, looked up at his entrance.

"Good morning, my dear. The post has already arrived, and I've had a letter from Sophie!" she reported, brandishing it with a smile.

"Ah, how are things in Paris?" Harry asked as he headed towards the sideboard.

"She says that rehearsals for *Figaro* are going well, and Sara is actually enjoying the experience of watching the company put their production together."

Harry lifted the lid off the nearest chafing dish, pleased to see that it did in fact contain kedgeree. He served himself a generous portion, moved on to eggs and sausage. "I hope she and Rob are finding time to enjoy their honeymoon, all the same."

"Oh, yes—they've been to Maxim's and the Eiffel Tower. And the three of them go riding in the Bois de Boulogne in the afternoon."

"Sounds positively idyllic." Harry carried his plate over to the table, sat down, and poured himself a cup of coffee from the silver service.

"There's a letter for you as well," Lady Tresilian observed, pushing the tray towards him.

Harry picked up the envelope, smiled when he saw the direction and the now-familiar hand. Breaking the seal, he extracted the folded pages and began to read.

May had settled into Kent with relative ease; he suspected that the presence of her sister had been a factor. They had apparently been close as children, before their respective marriages had distanced them from each other, physically and emotionally. Now, as widows, they were rediscovering their earlier bond, and Harry was glad of it. May had never made a close female friend during her time in St. Perran.

The overall tone of her letter was brisk and friendly, without the least trace of sentimentality or regret for what was past. Harry thought that, eventually, he would come to share those feelings and think of May more as a friend than as his former mistress. Perhaps that day was even closer than he thought, because he felt more of a gentle nostalgia on reading her words than a heart-rending anguish over her absence. Which meant, he supposed, that they'd made the right choice—for both of them—to move on.

"Is everything . . . all right?"

Harry glanced up from his letter to find his mother regarding him with mingled curiosity and concern. He did not doubt that she'd noticed that his letter had come from Kent, but

May would never be one of his mother's favorite topics, so he only smiled before tucking the letter away. "Just fine, Mother."

"I'm glad to hear it," Lady Tresilian said, after a moment.

Harry busied himself with his breakfast; the kedgeree was delicious. "Any other news, from Paris or elsewhere?"

His mother rallied at once, "Well, now that you mention it, my dear, I thought I'd let you know I've found a new tenant—short-term—for Tidewater Cottage. You know it's stood empty since Mrs. Permewan passed away last summer."

"Weren't you thinking of selling it?" he asked.

"Briefly. But I decided it made more sense simply to have it repainted and refurbished so it could be let out again. According to the land agent, quite a number of people are looking for summer places by the sea. And they could hardly improve upon Cornwall for that!"

Harry shrugged as he poured cream into his coffee. "Well, it was your property—yours and Father's—so do as you like with it. Who's the new tenant?"

"A widow, by the name of Mrs. Angove," Lady Tresilian replied. "She wants to stay in it for at least part of the spring, and she would be coming down at Easter—that's about a fortnight hence. I've already written to accept her terms, and I hope you won't mind calling on her once she's in residence, dear, and make her feel welcome in St. Perran . . ."

Harry smothered a sigh. So it was to begin again, now that May was gone and he was "fancy-free." Well, with any luck, the widow might turn out to be as elderly as the late Mrs. Permewan and have a confirmed taste for solitude! Still, there was no harm in being polite or even hospitable. "Naturally, Mother, I will show Mrs. Angove every courtesy during her stay."

~

LONDON, *two days later...*

. . .

Hers. Her own little cottage by the sea! Rose hugged the letter to her in something close to ecstasy.

For a few blessed weeks, she'd have all the peace and privacy her heart could wish. No crowds, no limelight, no endless scrutiny of her every word and movement. No unwanted admirers, importuning her with expensive gifts and highly questionable proposals. She felt like a schoolgirl on the brink of holidays— free to do as she pleased and to go wherever she chose, to be *Rose* again and not the all too public figure circumstances had forced her to become.

If only she could truly be *herself*.

The thought sobered her at once. But she'd turned the idea over and over in her head these last few weeks, before arriving reluctantly at the conclusion that there was no other way for this to work. Biting her lip, she turned to face her reflection in the cheval glass.

Her hair cascaded in loose ringlets over her shoulders, golden-red even by gaslight and far too distinctive and recognizable. That would have to be the first thing to go.

Frowning, she held out a lock of it for closer inspection. Blonde would still be too noticeable, and auburn far too dramatic—no, what she needed was a plain, nondescript brown, of a shade that wouldn't look too jarring against her fair skin. And she'd have to darken her brows and lashes as well. For once she was glad that she had brown eyes, rather than the more unusual blue or green, which would make it far easier to pose as a natural brunette.

Fortunately, her disguise need not be much more elaborate than that. She had no distinguishing marks to conceal upon her face or any part of her that would be visible to strangers. Besides, she knew from experience that people tended to overlook the ordinary rather than the hideous. To that end, she'd selected the simplest and least conspicuous garments for her holiday, clothes that would help her to blend in rather than stand out. Thank heaven Society accounted Cornwall such a backwater, though Rose knew of only one other place as lovely!

A knock sounded on her door. "Mrs. Langley! Fifteen minutes to curtain."

"Thank you!" she called back in acknowledgment.

Tucking the letter away in a drawer, she returned to the mirror and, as was her practice, tried to *think* herself into the part she would play tonight. She only hoped that, when the time came, she could enact the role of "Mrs. Angove" every bit as convincingly . . .

THANK YOU

Thank you for reading *The Heiress Brides*! I hope you enjoyed it.

Would you like to know when my next book is available?

*You can find out by signing up for my newsletter at http://www.pamelasherwood.com.

*Or follow me on Twitter at https://twitter.com/pamela_sherwood

*Or like my FacebookPage at https://www.facebook.com/PamelaSherwoodAuthor.

Reviews help readers find books, so I hope you will consider leaving a review at your venue of choice. I appreciate all reviews, whether positive or negative.

The Heiress Brides contains two previously published novellas: *A Scandal in Newport*, which takes place after *Waltz with a Stranger*, and *A Wedding in Cornwall*, which follows *A Song at Twilight*. Amy Newbold and Thomas Sheridan were the secondary couple in *Waltz with a Stranger*, the story of Aurelia Newbold and James Trelawney. Sophie Tresilian and Robin Pendarvis were the primary couple in *A Song at Twilight*.

To see how it all began, read on for excerpts from both novels in **The Heiress Series**!

WALTZ WITH A STRANGER: EXCERPT

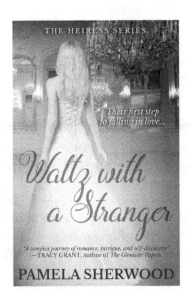

AVAILABLE FROM BLUE CASTLE PUBLISHING

A man who never expected to inherit. A woman who never expected to wed. A choice that pits their honor against their hearts.

Scarred and lame after a riding accident, shy heiress Aurelia

Newbold is resigned to her wallflower status—until a handsome, gallant stranger draws her into a secret waltz and awakens long-buried desires. A year later, a newly confident Aurelia returns to London, hoping to meet her mysterious partner again... only to find that he has since acquired a title, an estate, and a beautiful fiancee. And the lucky lady just happens to be Aurelia's beloved twin sister.

~

CHAPTER ONE

She was a Phantom of delight,
When first she gleamed upon my sight...
A dancing shape, an image gay
To haunt, to startle, and waylay.
--WILLIAM WORDSWORTH, "She Was a Phantom of
   Delight"

LONDON, MAY 1890

IF SOCIAL SUCCESS was measured by the number of guests the hostess could cram into a limited amount of space, then Lady Talbot's ball honoring her daughter's betrothal to Viscount Maitland's heir was an unqualified triumph. James Trelawney wished he could be properly appreciative of such an achievement, instead of counting the minutes until he could make his escape. Another half-hour or so before the break for supper--perhaps he could slip away then.

"I see you made it, after all," a familiar voice remarked at his shoulder.

"Thomas." Despite the crowd hemming them in, James managed to turn his head to smile at his closest friend. "Well, Jess is my cousin--and my aunt can be very persuasive."

"So she can. Pity the army doesn't recruit women--Lady Talbot would make a formidable general. Here," Thomas

Sheridan held out a brimming champagne flute. "This should help."

"Do I look that uncomfortable?" James took a sip of the excellent wine.

"Like the proverbial fish out of water. Wishing yourself back in Cornwall?"

"When am I not?" James sipped his champagne again, thinking longingly of the open spaces and crisp, salty air of his home county. "I only come up to London when I must. Frankly, I don't know how you stand it, Thomas. You're an artist, for God's sake!"

His friend's eyes glinted. "There's beauty and grace to be found even here, James. Or perhaps I should say, *especially* here."

He meant women, of course--being something of a connoisseur. Amused, James surveyed the ladies gracing the ballroom. Most were attractive, he supposed, but there were lovely women to be found in Cornwall too. He was just about to point that out to Thomas, when the musicians struck up a waltz. The couples assembled on the floor began to move, the ladies' jewels glittering beneath the radiance of the gas-lit chandelier, their pastel skirts belling out behind them with each whirling turn. He glimpsed his cousin Jessica, all in white, floating rapturously in the arms of her betrothed.

A flash of vivid blue among the preponderance of white and pink caught his eye. Idly, his gaze followed the motion of that swirling gown, traveled upward to the wearer's face...

He ceased to breathe, as if a fist had driven the air from his lungs. Beauty. Grace. *Oh, yes.*

Eyes as blue as her gown, the color of sunlit summer skies; a creamy complexion blushed with rose; smiling lips of a deeper rose hue; and a glory of spun-gold hair, bright as any coronet.

"Thomas." His voice sounded husky, even faraway. "Thomas, who's that--in blue?"

His friend followed the line of his gaze, stilled abruptly. "Ah. *La Belle Américaine.*"

An odd note in that cool, cultured voice, like the faintest

crack in a bell. James glanced at his friend, but saw only Thomas's habitual expression of ironic detachment.

"Miss Amelia Newbold," Sheridan continued. "Amy, to her closest friends. The latest heiress to cross the Atlantic and lay siege to our damp, foggy island."

"An heiress. From America?" That might explain her vivacity; English misses tended to carry themselves more demurely, with downcast eyes and half-smiles reminiscent of La Giaconda. Miss Newbold looked as though she was on the verge of laughter-- enchantingly so.

"New York, to be precise. The father's in shipping, I understand. Miss Newbold arrived in London with her mother and sister about two months ago and proceeded to cut a swathe through our susceptible young--and not so young--aristocrats. I've heard she'll accept nothing less than a peer. They don't lack for ambition, these Americans! And as you see," Thomas nodded towards the waltzing couples, "she already has Kelmswood in her toils."

James glanced at Miss Newbold's partner, noticing him for the first time: a tall, athletically built young man whose dark good looks seemed the perfect foil for the American girl's golden beauty. The thought gave him no pleasure whatsoever. "An earl, isn't he? I suppose they're as good as betrothed, then."

"I wouldn't bet on that." Thomas's mouth crooked. "Glyndon's entered the lists as well."

James's brows rose. "Good God, really?" Viscount Glyndon, Thomas's cousin, was heir to the Duke of Harford. "How do their Graces feel about that?"

"My uncle and aunt are maintaining a well-bred silence on the subject. However, I doubt their plans for my cousin's future include an American bride."

Having met the duke and duchess, James was inclined to agree with his friend. Not that it mattered--could matter--to him: the likes of Amelia Newbold were out of his humble star. He made himself look away from her and her handsome, eligible partner. "I think I'll go and get some air. If you'll excuse me?"

Thomas relieved him of his now-empty flute. "Of course, old fellow."

James threaded his way through the crowd towards the French windows, standing open to the warm spring night. Just as he was about to step onto the terrace, a raucous male laugh assailed his ears. A raucous, all-too-familiar male laugh.

Damn, and damn again. Gritting his teeth, James ventured a glance onto the terrace, saw several men leaning against the balustrade in a haze of cigar smoke. In their midst he spotted a familiar blond head, a heavy profile: his cousin Gerald, Viscount Alston.

He ought to have expected this; Aunt Judith was the family peacemaker. If she'd invited one of her nephews to attend Jessica's betrothal ball, she would certainly invite the other, despite knowing that he and Gerald met as seldom as possible. They both preferred it that way.

Memories stirred, a dark tide with a deadly undertow. James forced them away, turned from the doors. The conservatory-- he'd go there instead. Even if other guests had sought refuge in the same place, they could hardly be less congenial company than Gerald and his cronies.

But, at first glance, the conservatory appeared to be deserted. Moonlight poured in through the glass-paneled walls, bathing the plants and stone benches in an otherworldly glow. Loosening his collar, James inhaled the warm, jasmine-scented air and felt himself relax for the first time that evening.

Hands clasped behind him, he strolled along the nearest walkway. Feathery ferns, sinuous vines, potted palms... he could not identify more than a few of the more exotic species, but it scarcely mattered: here, at last, were peace and tranquility. Then he rounded a corner, came to a halt at the sight of the figure standing in the middle of the conservatory, the moonlight frosting her golden hair and casting a silvery sheen upon the skirts of her blue ball gown. Her eyes were closed, her slim form swaying gently in time to the waltz music drifting in from the ballroom.

James wondered if he'd lost his mind. Hadn't he just seen her mere moments ago, dancing in the arms of an earl? Then, looking more closely, he saw that the shade of her gown was closer to turquoise than azure, her hair dressed a touch less elaborately: subtle differences but telling nonetheless. What had Thomas said? "She and her mother and her sister..."

He must have made some sound, some movement, because the girl suddenly froze like a deer scenting a hunter, apprehension radiating from every inch of her.

James spoke quickly, seeking to reassure her. "Pardon me, Miss Newbold. It is Miss Newbold, is it not?"

Aurelia fought down a rush of panic and an irrational urge to flee--for all the good it would do her. The stranger's voice was deep and pleasant, with a faint burr she could not place. She wondered if he was as attractive as he sounded; the thought made her even more reluctant to turn around.

But it would be rude not to acknowledge his presence. Keeping her face averted, she nodded. "I am Aurelia Newbold."

"Miss Aurelia," he amended. "My name's Trelawney. Again, I ask your pardon. I could not help but stare--no one told me that you and your sister were identical twins."

Aurelia swallowed, knowing she could no longer delay the inevitable. Best to get it over with, as quickly as possible "We are twins, sir. But--no longer identical."

She turned around, letting him see the whole of her face now--thinner and paler than Amy's, despite their maid's skilled application of cosmetics. But no amount of paint or powder could disguise the scar that ran along the left side of her hairline before curving sharply across her cheekbone like a reversed letter *J*. She forced herself to meet Mr. Trelawney's eyes, even as her stomach knotted in dread over what she would see.

And there it was--that flash of pity in his eyes; dark eyes, in a strongly handsome face that recalled portraits of dashing adventurers and soldiers of fortune. At least they held no distaste or revulsion: a small mercy. Or perhaps he was simply better at hiding them.

"A riding accident." she said tersely, anticipating the question he was trying not to ask. "Three years ago. It's left me with a limp as well."

"I am sorry." His voice was kind. "That must be difficult to bear. Do you need to sit down? I could escort you back to the ballroom, find you a chair."

Aurelia shook her head. "That won't be necessary, sir. I just-- came to admire the conservatory." And to escape all the stares, whether curious or pitying. She'd have preferred to stay behind in their suite at Claridge's tonight, but Amy had refused to attend this ball without her. Beautiful Amy, who looked the way *she* had used to look.

"I see." And as his dark eyes continued to study her, Aurelia had the uncomfortable feeling that Mr. Trelawney did indeed see.

"They fade, you know," he said, almost abruptly. "Scars. When I was a boy, I knew a man who'd served in the Crimea and had a saber cut down one side of his face. Many saw it as a badge of honor. In later years, some even thought it made him look distinguished."

"Scars on a man may be distinguished, Mr. Trelawney," Aurelia said, more sharply than she intended. "On a woman, they're merely ugly. And there was nothing--honorable or heroic about the way I acquired mine." *Merely stupid.*

His brows drew together. "Surely you need not be defined by your scars, Miss Newbold."

She felt her lips twist in a brittle smile. "It's hard not to be, when they're the first things about me that people notice."

"But you are under no obligation to accept their valuation of you. And would *you* judge another solely on the basis of injury or illness?"

He spoke mildly, but she heard the faint rebuke in his voice, nonetheless. Flushing, she looked away, ashamed of her outburst. She'd thought herself resigned, if not reconciled, to her disfigurement; what was it about this man that unsettled her so?

"I would hope not, especially now. Pardon me, sir, I let my--disappointment get the best of me. A graceless thing to do, and I'm sorry for it. If you'll excuse me, I'll return to the ballroom." Still not looking at him, she turned towards the conservatory doors.

"Wait." The urgency in his voice stopped her in her tracks. "Miss Newbold, may I have this dance?"

Aurelia whipped her head around, astonished. "Dance? Pray do not mock me, sir."

Dark eyes gazed steadily into hers. "I have never been more serious in my life. You have a fine sense of rhythm--I noticed that when first I saw you. Are you fond of the waltz?"

"Well, yes," she admitted, after a moment; there'd been a time when she loved nothing better than to whirl about the floor in her partner's arms. "That is, I was before. But my limp--"

"A limp is surely no worse than two left feet--and the latter affliction has not prevented quite a number of people from dancing tonight."

A breath of unwilling laughter escaped her; Mr. Trelawney's eyes seemed to warm at the sound. He held out his hand. "I do not ask this out of mockery--or pity," he added, with a perception that surprised her. "Will you not indulge me? We need not return to the ballroom--we can have our dance here, unseen, among the flowers. Unless you find it too physically taxing?'

He'd just handed her the perfect excuse. All she had to do was plead fatigue or discomfort, and Mr. Trelawney, gentleman that he was, would surely let her retire and not importune her further. Instead, she stepped forward--and placed her hand in his.

He smiled at her and her knees wanted to buckle; she made herself stand fast and look him in the eye. She could feel the warmth of his hand through the evening gloves they both wore, and smell his cologne, an appealing blend of citrus and clove. Then he drew her to him, his hand resting lightly on the small of her back, and led her into their dance.

Her first steps were halting, hesitant, and she felt her face flaming anew, but Mr. Trelawney took her clumsiness in stride, adjusting his movements to hers. A few more bars and Aurelia found herself dancing more easily, as if some purely physical memory had taken over, leaving her mind free to concentrate on the beauty of the moonlit conservatory and the light pressure of Mr. Trelawney's arms enfolding her as gently as if she were made of porcelain.

Together, they waltzed along the paved walkways, around benches and garden beds, beneath the light of the moon and stars. With each circling turn, Aurelia felt her spirits rise, a sensation that had become as alien to her as a man's touch. Mr. Trelawney danced with an easy assurance that seemed of a piece with his forthright manner and confident air. No other man she'd waltzed with had ever made her feel this safe--not Papa, not Andrew... not even Charlie.

That last realization was so startling that she almost stumbled; Mr. Trelawney steadied her at once, concern in his eyes. Aurelia summoned a smile that surprised her as much as it did her partner, and they waltzed on, whirling back towards the center of the conservatory and the pool of moonlight on the tiled floor.

The music ended, the last chords quavering into silence, and Mr. Trelawney swirled them both to a stop. Aurelia stifled a pang of regret at how quickly the time had passed.

"Thank you," she said, and meant it. She was slightly breathless, and her bad leg twinged after the unaccustomed exercise; it would be worse in the morning, but she felt not even a particle of regret.

He gave her that knee-weakening smile again. "The pleasure was mine, Miss Newbold."

The sound of a throat being discreetly cleared drew their attention to the doorway, where a liveried footman now stood. "Mr. Trelawney?"

His brows rose inquiringly. "Yes?"

"Lady Talbot wishes to speak with you, sir. In the supper room."

"Ah. Tell her I'll be along straightaway."

"Very good, sir." The footman withdrew at once.

Mr. Trelawney turned back to Aurelia. "Pardon me, Miss Newbold, but I must wait upon my aunt. May I escort you back to the ballroom now?"

She shook her head. "No, thank you. I'd like to remain in the conservatory a while longer." Solitude would give her the chance to recover her poise--and invisibility.

"As you wish." But he lingered a moment longer. "Thank you for the waltz. Perhaps--we might attempt it again, sometime?"

Aurelia swallowed, deliberately not allowing herself to dwell on that possibility. "Perhaps we might, at that. Good evening, Mr. Trelawney."

He raised her hand briefly to his lips. "And to you, Miss Newbold."

He bowed and strode from the conservatory. Much to Aurelia's vexation, her traitorous gaze followed him, long after he had disappeared into the crowded ballroom.

A SONG AT TWILIGHT: EXCERPT

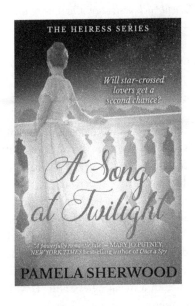

AVAILABLE FROM BLUE CASTLE PUBLISHING

She has everything she's ever dreamed of—except the man who broke her heart.

Sophie Tresilian is the toast of Europe, a silver-voiced singer whose star is on the rise. Though desired by countless men, she lost her heart years ago to Robin Pendarvis.... but secrets from the past tore them apart. His sudden reappearance turns her world upside-down, reviving all the old pain—and all the old passion. Unable to deny the love that still burns between them, they will risk everything to be together again. But will the scandal that blighted their past destroy their future as well?

~

CHAPTER ONE

O, call back yesterday! Bid time return.
—SHAKESPEARE, *Richard II*

LONDON, July 1896

HE'D BEEN A FOOL TO COME, but he couldn't have stayed away if his life depended on it.

All around him, Robin could hear the rustle of programmes, the faint coughs and murmurs as the audience settled in before the performance. Down in the pit, violins lilted and cellos thrummed as the orchestra tuned up its instruments. The concert had sold out quickly--he'd been fortunate to secure a prime seat in one of the lower tiers with a clear view of the stage. But even the galleries and balconies were full tonight.

He smoothed out his programme with hands that shook only slightly, read the lines of print over and over again until the words ran together in a meaningless blur. David Cherwell, the promising Welsh tenor, and Sophia Tresilian--one of the finest young sopranos in recent memory--performing together for one night only at the prestigious Albert Hall.

Sophia. The name seemed to belong to some glamorous stranger. In Cornwall, among those who knew her best, she was just Sophie. Sometimes "Snip" to her brother Harry. "Lark" to her sister Cecily. And to Robin himself... He pushed the thought away, reminding himself that he'd lost the right to call her anything at all four years ago. Lost it, renounced it, thrown it away... and for the best. What could he have offered her then but heartache and ruin?

And now here she was--celebrated, adored, at the start of a brilliant career. And here *he* was, watching and waiting. To see all that radiant promise fulfilled. To comfort himself with the knowledge that he'd done the right thing. And for one more reason, that he could not, dared not, put into words yet.

One way or another, tonight would tell the tale.

The house lights dimmed and the orchestra launched into a brisk overture that Robin barely heeded because his attention was fixed on the stage. As the last flourish sounded, he saw the slender figure walk out to take her place before them all.

Not tall, Sophie, but she carried herself with a poise that made her appear so. Stage lights caught the coppery glints in her dark hair, shone on the smooth ivory heart of her face, the slim column of her throat, rising from the décolleté neckline of her gown--a gown the color of midnight, almost void of ornament, severe but becoming. She'd worn white the first time he saw her, trimmed with a froth of lace as fine as snowflakes. A young girl's dress, artless and unsophisticated, but even then the woman had begun to emerge. And here she stood now, the blossom to the bud, so beautiful it made him ache.

And not just him. He sensed the heightened awareness around him, the way so many of the men in his vicinity seemed to come to a point. Like hunting dogs catching the first whiff of game, or orchid hunters sighting a rare, elusive bloom.

Unseen, the piano rippled out the introduction, the somber chords echoing through the hall. Onstage, Sophie raised her head and began to sing.

"Music for a while, Shall all your cares beguile..."

Purcell--she'd always had a fondness for that composer's songs. Her voice held the same purity he remembered, but with an added richness, the patina of training and experience. Caught between pride and pain, Robin sat motionless and listened, absorbing every note.

How long had it been, since he'd first heard her sing?

Five years ago, this past December. A lifetime ago...

ACKNOWLEDGMENTS

PUTTING TOGETHER a novella collection was a challenge I hadn't yet tackled, and in characteristic fashion, I found myself obsessing over minutiae. So I thank everyone who helped keep me sane during that time, my family foremost among them!

I would also like to thank Amanda L. Matthews for the beautiful cover that works so well for both stories. And my beta readers for always being willing to look over what I've written. And the self-publishing community that has taught me so much. And my readers, of course!

ALSO BY PAMELA SHERWOOD

The Lyons Pride

The Advent of Lady Madeline

Devices & Desires

Twelfth Night

Epiphany

Intimate Delights (collection)

A Lyons in Winter (box set)

A Bride by Michaelmas (forthcoming)

Women & Wine (forthcoming)

The Heiress Series

Waltz with a Stranger

A Scandal in Newport

A Song at Twilight

A Wedding in Cornwall

The Heiress Brides (collection)

Short Story Collections

Awakened and Other Enchanted Tales

ABOUT THE AUTHOR

PAMELA SHERWOOD is an avid reader of multiple genres (horror excepted) and aspires to be a prolific writer of multiple genres (again, horror excepted). In a previous life, she earned a doctorate in English literature, specializing in the Romantic and Victorian periods, and taught college-level literature and writing courses. At present, she writes historical romance and fantasy. Her books have received starred reviews in *Booklist* and *Library Journal*, and *Waltz with a Stranger*, her debut novel, won the Laurel Wreath Award for Best Historical Romance in 2013. *Devices & Desires*, Book One in The Lyons Pride series, won the 2017 Golden Quill for Best Historical. Pamela lives with her family in Southern California, where she continues to read voraciously, spin plots, and straddle genres to tell the kind of stories she loves.

Visit her on the web at http://pamelasherwood.com, facebook. com/PamelaSherwoodAuthor, and twitter.com/pamela_sherwood